They stopped in front of her door, and Shondra looked up from finding her keys to thank him for the evening.

Before she could get any words out of her mouth, he was pulling her close.

The next thing she knew, she was flattened against his chest and his soft, firm lips were on hers.

A flash of hunger shot through her in his strong, purposeful embrace. Shondra gave herself a moment to enjoy his kiss—soft and heated with just the tiniest flick of tongue—before she pulled away, breathless.

"Connor," she said when she finally regained her voice. "Thank you for dinner and a really fun evening. But as much as I'd like to continue where we just left off, I really don't think it's wise for us to get involved. After all, you're my boss."

Books by Robyn Amos

Kimani Romance

Enchanting Melody
Sex and the Single Braddock

Kimani Arabesque

Promise Me
I Do
Private Lies
Into the Night
True Blue

ROBYN AMOS

worked a multitude of day jobs while pursuing a career in writing. After graduating from college with a degree in psychology, she married her real-life romantic hero, a genuine rocket scientist. Finally, she was able to live her dream of writing full-time. Since her first book was published in 1997, Robyn has written tales of romantic comedy and suspense for several publishers, including Kensington Books, Harlequin and HarperCollins. A native of the Washington, D.C., metropolitan area, Robyn currently resides in Odenton, Maryland.

Sex and the Single Braddock

ROBYN AMOS

KIMANI™
ROMANCE

This book is for Adrianne, A.C. and Brenda.
It was a pleasure working with you, ladies.

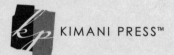

KIMANI PRESS™

ISBN-13: 978-0-373-86081-4
ISBN-10:   0-373-86081-1

SEX AND THE SINGLE BRADDOCK

Dear Reader,

Participating in a continuity series can be both a lot of fun and a really big challenge. The most fun I had writing *Sex and the Single Braddock* was getting to talk to three other extremely talented authors about how our books were going to fit together. Adrianne Byrd, A.C. Arthur and Brenda Jackson were so easy to work with and as a team we came up with some great ideas.

The most challenging part of writing this story was conquering unfamiliar territory. When I received the story line, I realized I was going to be writing about Texas oil wells, fancy sports cars and decadent escapades to exotic locations. These things were all new to me. Since I couldn't convince my husband to take me to Monte Carlo on a private jet, I had a lot of fun letting my imagination run wild.

I hope you enjoy reading about how Shondra and Connor find love despite the contrary demands of their families. It takes Shondra a while to learn that it's okay to let go of control and let new experiences happen. And this is definitely a lesson I learned for myself while working on *Sex and the Single Braddock*.

I love to hear from readers. E-mail me at robynamos@aol.com or visit me on the Web at www.robynamos.com.

Happy reading,

Robyn Amos

Chapter 1

Shondra Braddock navigated the narrow metal stairs leading down from the helipad. She was on an oil rig in the middle of the Gulf of Mexico. And it was hot.

She shook hands with the liaison from Stewart Industries who'd met her at the airport that morning. "And now I'll leave you in the capable hands of the crew," the young man said as he turned to leave.

Out of the jumble of workers milling about, an oil-stained man stepped forward. Other than the blond hair brushing his collar from under the hard hat, Shondra couldn't make out much. Hidden among the streaks of grime were a few patches of golden tan, a pair of ice-blue eyes and a smile containing the straightest white teeth she'd ever seen.

"I'll be showing you around." He gave her a sheepish grin. "I'd shake your hand, but…" He nodded to his oil-covered hands, which he continued to wipe on a rag. "Sorry about this. I had to do some emergency work on the bottomhole assembly. I didn't want to make you wait while I showered."

"Don't worry about it," she said, reaching out to shake his hand anyway. "I'm Shondra Braddock, the new chief compliance officer."

His fingers were strong and firm in hers, and Shondra felt a little jolt when their skin made contact. Deciding the ninety-degree heat was getting to her, she took the rag he offered and wiped her hands before passing it back.

Dressed like the others, he wore brown work pants and a shirt with C.J. stitched on the breast pocket. He'd ripped the sleeves off the shirt, revealing his tanned, muscular arms. Shondra forced herself not to drool. It was no secret that she had a thing for buff, working-class men, and something about this guy was pushing all of her buttons.

Once again blaming the heat, she forced her mind back to the business at hand. "It's nice to meet you…C.J.?"

He nodded, flashing her another grin worthy of a toothpaste ad. "Let me find you a hard hat, and we'll get this tour under way."

Less than a minute later C.J. returned carrying a yellow hard hat. Expecting him to hand it to her, Shondra found herself holding her breath as he reached out to settle it on her head himself. Lifting her chin to inspect his work, he nodded with approval. "Perfect fit."

Then he winked at her and Shondra felt a tingle shoot down her spine.

Before she could analyze whether or not he was flirting with her, C.J. was leading her down a narrow aisle. "Have you ever been on a jackup rig?" he called over his shoulder.

Shondra stopped cold, thinking he'd said something obscene. "A what!"

"You're standing on a Tarzan-class jackup rig. We drag it to the drilling site, drive the legs into the sea floor and then jack up the entire rig above the reach of hurricane waves. Once we strike oil, we'll cap the well, jack down the rig and drag it to the next site."

"I see," Shondra said. She had to pay better attention. It wasn't like her to let the proximity of a man she'd just met affect her this much.

As C.J. showed her around the rig, Shondra became convinced he was touching her more than was necessary—guiding her through narrow passageways with a hand on the small of her back or tugging gently on her wrist.

And she knew he was flirting with her when he asked, "What's a pretty girl like you doing working in oil?"

"Come on," she said. "I was born and raised in Texas. It's practically in my blood."

"And you're a chief compliance officer? That sounds very official. Do you enjoy that type of work?" His tone implied that he couldn't imagine that she would.

Shondra laughed. "I love everything about my job. I work best under pressure, the travel keeps me interested and, believe it or not, I enjoy the meticulous attention to detail that risk management and compliance require."

"Whoa." C.J. laughed at her. "Now you sound

like you're on a job interview. You can't really love all that paperwork, filing and forms…"

"I do and I think I'm going to really like working for Stewart Industries."

Her new job was shaping up to have everything she needed. She'd only been with the company for a week and before she could set up her desk, she'd jumped on a plane to Mexico to research compliance issues for a new drilling site.

That alone would've been enough to keep her interested, but this was more than just a job to her.

A chill tingled her skin despite the heat.

She had a mission that was both personal and deeply painful. So painful, Shondra had to carefully balance her emotions on the subject lest she crack her cool exterior and crumble to pieces on the spot.

Narrowing her gaze on C.J.'s back, she was able to keep her thoughts focused. It was up to her to find out all she could about Stewart Industries. This was a crucial task because her family believed someone within the company had a connection to her father's recent death.

When her father's former personal assistant received an anonymous call stating that Harmon Braddock's fatal car crash hadn't been an accident, Shondra couldn't sit back and wait for answers. Then they found evidence of a flight to Washington, D.C., and calls made the day of Harmon's death that traced back to the main switchboard of Stewart Industries—which made no sense. Her father's personal assistant, who knew everything about her father's business dealings, knew nothing about a connection to Stewart Industries. Clearly something wasn't right.

This information had left Shondra and her brothers, Malcolm and Tyson, with a lot of questions. For the time being, their mother, still deeply in mourning for her husband, was being kept out of the loop. At least until they had solid answers.

Her family needed to know the truth about Harmon Braddock's death, and Shondra had found a way to get on the inside at Stewart Industries. She'd called in a few favors and wrangled herself a position with the company.

She was good at what she did and the Braddock name carried a lot of weight in Houston. Even though she had her own agenda, she would do her job to the best of her abilities. Her pride wouldn't accept anything less.

After showing her the technical side of the rig

where all the hard work got done, C.J. took her to the crew's quarters, the cafeteria and the rec room.

Occasionally some of the roughnecks would ogle her openly. Shondra knew she was an attractive woman, but she didn't take the extra attention personally. She suspected some of these men hadn't seen a woman in weeks, which could account for their admiring stares. At least that was how she explained the heated looks she felt coming from her tour guide.

But if C.J. did have a bit of a crush on her, she could use it to her advantage and do some subtle probing about the company.

"I was hired by Carl Stewart," she said, dropping the name of the company's CEO. "Does he ever come down to the rig and see you guys?"

"Not too much," C.J. replied, and to Shondra's disappointment, he did not elaborate.

"I guess he's starting to pull back from some of the operations. It's my understanding that he's preparing to pass the title of CEO on to his son Connor," she prodded.

C.J. simply shrugged. "That's my understanding, too."

Shondra was puzzled. Up until then, C.J. had been chatty and forthcoming. Now he seemed to be holding back. Her initial research suggested that SI was really tight with information. If she couldn't even get an oil-rig worker to schmooze about the bigwigs, maybe SI really did have something to hide.

"I've never met Connor Stewart. What is he like as a boss?"

C.J. turned up the wattage on his winsome smile. "Are you nervous about meeting the company president?"

Shondra shook her head. "Overpaid suits with fancy titles don't scare me. Trust me, I've dealt with enough of those. My only concern is learning the ins and outs of this company so I can do my job effectively."

C.J. laughed. "Well, I'm sure that's all that really matters." He led her around a corner and stopped in front of a door. "I think that covers everything. We've got an empty office here where you can start reviewing the paperwork for the new site."

"Thanks for the tour." She reached out to shake C.J.'s hand. Once again, she took a moment to appreciate the firm grip of his strong, work-roughened hands.

She found herself wondering what all that

grime on his face was hiding. Though his features were smudged, she could tell they were well put together.

Shondra knew it was wrong to mix business with pleasure. But growing up in a household of overprotective men had nurtured her rebellious streak. Besides, it was more than likely she'd never see this man again. In a few hours she'd be on a plane back to Houston.

What would C.J. say if she asked him to join her in that empty office? He'd been eyeing her with those wicked blue eyes all afternoon. He'd probably say yes.

With a sigh, Shondra waved goodbye and ducked into the office alone. As usual, her rebellious streak never extended past her thoughts.

At the end of the day, Shondra was a good girl with a naughty imagination. She grew up under the heavy weight of expectation, and despite temptation, she couldn't bring herself to let anyone down.

The daughters of African-American families in prominent positions in politics did not make scandal. That made backroom romps with oil-rig workers strictly forbidden.

But she could daydream…

* * *

That evening, Connor Stewart reclined in the butter-soft leather seats on the company jet. A smile curved his lips as he watched a helicopter land on the airfield.

Shondra Braddock popped out of the aircraft, waving what looked like an airline ticket. She vigorously pointed toward the terminal.

Connor laughed out loud.

Her company escort shook his head and pointed toward the jet where Connor sat. Finally, clearly confused, Shondra began to approach the plane.

Her professional polish hadn't faded since he'd left her that afternoon. She wore trim tan slacks that molded her hips, a matching vest and a short-sleeved white blouse. Her long dark hair was pulled back from her face and fastened at her nape in a low ponytail.

Connor watched as she marched, briefcase in hand, up the steps to the plane. It was easy to appreciate her warm brown skin and her elegant beauty. Despite the attraction he'd felt between them from the start, she'd appeared unflappable. Well, he'd just see about that.

Shondra stepped through the curtain and

stopped dead in her tracks. Connor grinned wickedly.

Raising her brows, she said, "You could have told me you were Connor Stewart."

He stood to take her briefcase and pointed her toward the seat across from him. "I could have. But I wanted the chance to get to know you without wondering if you were just putting on a show for the boss. The last two people I took on that tour thought they were too good to rub elbows with the workers that make all of our jobs possible…at least until they were told who I was. Their employment didn't last long after that."

"Ah, so they never figured out that you're just an overpaid suit with a fancy title?"

Connor threw back his head and laughed. She *was* unflappable and *he* was charmed. "Touché. Although I have to say, even though I'm paid well, I think I'm worth it."

She leveled him with her gaze. "Of course you do."

"But I'll give you the other two. I do wear a lot of suits, and I guess my title is pretty fancy." Of course, he was hoping his father would stop dangling the CEO title over his head just to keep him in line. The old man needed to go ahead and retire as promised.

Shondra looked him over. "Speaking of suits, it's nice to see that you clean up well."

Connor shifted in his seat under her intent stare. He suddenly felt like he was no longer in control of this situation. "Thanks."

"So that oil-covered getup was just for my benefit?"

"Not exactly. I met you covered in oil because I really was working on the bottomhole assembly," he answered.

"A man who's not afraid to get his hands dirty—impressive. And, C.J.?"

"Connor James. C.J. is what the crew calls me when I'm on a rig. It helps them remember I'm just one of the team."

Shondra nodded. "So I take it that I passed your little test, then?"

Connor simply smiled.

Shondra looked around, taking in the luxury interior of the private jet. "Then riding back to Houston with the company president must be my prize. What happens to those poor suckers who don't pass? Do you throw them in the baggage hold?"

He found himself laughing yet again. He had to remind himself he was on a business trip, not a date.

"No, if you don't pass, we just drop you in the ocean and let you swim for the border."

"I guess I'd better be on my best behavior then. Sounds like you're hard to please."

"Maybe. But you don't have anything to worry about. Your reputation and résumé are outstanding."

"Yes, but that clearly wasn't enough for you," she said, referring to his little test. "Are you always so distrustful?"

"I wouldn't say it's a matter of trust. Just experience. Haven't you met someone who looked perfect on paper but couldn't live up to their own hype?"

Shondra nodded.

"Then you should understand. I like to rely on what I can see and hear for myself."

And he was more than a little impressed with Shondra. She was even better in person than she was on paper. Not only did she have a genuine passion for her work, but she had a natural charm that had won over everyone she'd met on the rig. Himself especially.

It wasn't unusual for him to pour on the charm to put his employees at ease, but he'd found himself going overboard with Shondra. Something about her made him react as a man first and employer second. He'd never let that happen before.

Meeting women came easy to Connor. Finding one that could hold his attention was nearly impossible. Once he weeded out the gold diggers, he was usually left with women who were either brainless or vapid.

It wasn't lost on him that he was in the presence of that rare find who was intelligent, quick-witted and unfazed by money or position. And all that aside…she was hot.

He'd never dated a black woman, but that had more to do with opportunity than anything else. Everything about Shondra was sexy. From the husky tease of her voice to her fit and firm curves.

But there were obvious obstacles in his path. Not the least of which was that he was Shondra's boss. He had to tread lightly, because if she didn't share his attraction, he could find himself in the middle of a sexual harassment incident. His father would love that.

But he had a feeling that the attraction was

mutual. At least that was the vibe he'd gotten when he'd been streaked in oil and wearing his work clothes. In that last moment before they'd said goodbye there was…*something* in the air between them.

She was in sassy mode now, using her acerbic wit to make him pay for trying to trick her. But earlier…there had definitely been some tension.

Maybe she had a thing for the working man. She'd already said she was impressed by a guy who wasn't afraid to get his hands dirty.

Connor shifted uncomfortably in his seat again. Thankfully, Shondra's attention was caught up with the flight attendant discussing their dinner options.

He had to pull it together. His father had made him promise that his phase of youthful rebellion was well in the past, and that Stewart Industries would be his only priority.

That made having his way with Shondra on the sofa bed to his left strictly off-limits.

He smiled at Shondra from across the table. Unfortunately, Connor had never been able to resist making his wicked thoughts a reality.

It was just a matter of time.

* * *

Shondra slipped into her condo and dropped her briefcase on the floor. This could be a problem. She was not supposed to have waking fantasies about buttoned-up blonds in expensive suits—especially when they turned up in the form of her boss.

Her taste normally ran to ranch hands and construction workers. There was something about a blue collar that she found very sexy. The bigger the muscles the better. Plus, it didn't hurt that it was an easy way to get a rise out of her family.

But getting involved with Connor Stewart went way beyond subtle rebellion. Shondra got a queasy feeling in the pit of her stomach when she thought about how her brothers would react. She'd like to hope that their feelings would have more to do with his family business than the fact that Connor was white, but she really couldn't be sure.

And now wasn't the time to put Malcolm and Tyson's progressive thinking to the test. Her family was grieving and everyone needed to pull together. This was Shondra's opportunity to step up and prove she was her brothers' equal.

She was a big girl. She could handle her

libido. What mattered most was that she had a job to do. Two in fact, because the compliance work had to be done, and she wouldn't sacrifice her professional reputation for an investigation that might not turn up anything.

When Harmon Braddock died, everything in Shondra's world came to a halt. Their family hadn't been perfect, but no one had expected it to be ripped apart by a devastating car accident. The past month had been like living inside a bubble. She watched the world like a bystander—no one could get in and she couldn't get out.

As Shondra struggled to come to terms with her father's death, her family got word that his crash may not have been an accident.

It shocked Shondra to think someone might have killed her father…but, somehow, the anonymous message rang true. Politicians couldn't please everyone, so it was conceivable that Harmon Braddock had made some enemies during his climb from Senator Cayman's legal counsel to congressman.

Shondra felt, in her heart, that Harmon Braddock had been a good man. And for many years he'd been popular with his constituents. But the family observed his gradual change as years passed. As his hours away from home grew, he became more the political stereotype, working more for corporate interest groups than for the people. It was this change that eventually forced Malcolm out of their father's footsteps.

When Malcolm and their father became estranged, the Braddock family began to grow apart. And it broke Shondra's heart that it took losing their father to reunite the family. In the past month they'd all begun to lean on each other again. Then, once more, things started unraveling.

First, her father's assistant, Gloria Kingsley, had found a mysterious number on Harmon's phone logs that traced back to Stewart Industries. Gloria had no knowledge or record of any official business between Harmon and SI. And what was up with Harmon's credit card bill showing a plane ticket to Washington, D.C., on the day he died? Gloria always booked his travel. So why not this one? She received a call implying that Harmon had been murdered, which also tracked back to the multimillion-dollar oil company.

With these new events, Shondra found her purpose again. Investigating her father's death brought her out of her bubble.

Finally she had something to do besides cry.

Realizing that she'd been standing in the foyer lost in a reverie, Shondra picked up her briefcase and headed for her bedroom.

Fueled by the thought of a relaxing bubble bath, Shondra picked up speed, only to come to a startled halt as her foot squished into a brown mess just inside her door.

"Lisa! Lisa, have you been bringing your dogs to the house again?"

Within a few seconds Lisa appeared in her doorway. "Oh shoot, I thought I'd found all of Muffin's little presents. I'll clean that up for you."

Rolling her eyes, Shondra kicked off her flat sling-backs. "And you owe me a new pair of shoes. *These* are now yours."

Lisa, now on her knees scrubbing at the stain, looked up incredulously through her veil of micro braids. "Are you kidding? It's just a little dog poop. It cleans right off."

"But the memory lingers. Girl, are your braids too tight? You promised me that you'd stop bringing those dogs to the house. You're lucky I don't charge you extra rent for all the cockadoos and peekachoos you have running around here."

Lisa sat up. "They're called *cockapoos* and *peekapoos*. And I *had* to bring Muffin here…just for the afternoon. The air conditioner at the shelter broke, and we each had to bring an animal home with us until it was fixed."

Shondra sighed and stretched out on her bed. Her roommate and best friend since college was a little off. They'd both graduated with degrees in law, but late last year Lisa quit her job with a prominent Houston firm to "find her passion." And for the past month, her passion had been walking dogs for a ritzy dog kennel downtown.

Shondra couldn't relate. She'd known what she'd wanted to do for a living since she was five. But as long as Lisa made rent, who was she to judge?

"There. Looks like it never happened." Lisa stood, brushing herself off. "How was your first business trip on the new job?"

Shondra sank back into her pillows. "It was really fun, actually. I got to fly back in the company jet with the president."

"Of the United States?"

Shondra leveled a hard stare at her friend. "Of course not. Of Stewart Industries."

Lisa ditched her cleaning supplies and sat on

the corner of the bed. "Wow. Private jet, huh? Maybe I got out of law too soon."

"It's never too late, my friend," Shondra said hopefully.

"Nope," Lisa finally said, shaking her head so her braids rattled. "It's better to be happy than rich."

Shondra grinned. "You know, it doesn't have to be either-or. Is dog walking really making you happy?"

Lisa shrugged. "I'm not saying I'll be doing this for the rest of my life. I'm still searching. I just think you can't make your mind up about something until you've tried it."

Shondra knew her friend was talking about careers, but she couldn't help applying that theory to her love life. Despite it being against her better judgment, or maybe because of it, over the course of the week, Shondra found herself looking around the office for Connor.

Part of her had hoped they would be running into each other regularly, but no such luck. By Thursday evening Shondra had convinced herself that this was fate's way of telling her to keep her head down and focus on the tasks at hand.

Which was why Connor caught her completely off guard when he called her at home.

"I'd like to take you out to dinner tomorrow night," he said.

Shondra's jaw dropped as she fumbled to find something to say. "Um, to talk about business?"

She heard his warm laugh and could just picture those white teeth glinting. "Not really."

Say no, she coached herself. "No…problem. Pick me up at eight."

Chapter 2

Shondra paced the foyer at a quarter to eight.

"Sit down," Lisa called from the living room sofa in front of their large arched window. "I can't remember the last time I've seen you this nervous before a date."

"Probably because I'm making a big mistake," she muttered to herself.

"What?"

"Nothing."

Inhaling another deep breath, she tried to make herself relax. No, this dinner didn't have to mean anything more than a meal between colleagues. Besides, it was another opportunity to find out more about the company and the man she worked for.

So, she reassured herself, this was not a blatantly reckless act designed to indulge her carnal desires. This was a necessary step in her investigation.

Shondra bit her lip. It was a stretch, but God forbid she had to explain herself, it might fly.

"He's here." Lisa slammed her bowl of spicy Szechuan chicken on the coffee table. "Girrrl, you didn't tell me this guy is loa-ded."

Shondra snapped to attention. "I—I—how can you tell?"

"In all the time I've known you, you've never dated a guy who drove anything better than rusty pickups or ten-year-old sedans. Your last guy was so broke, he would show up in a cab and then make you pay. Now all of a sudden, *this* one shows up driving a Bugatti Veyron."

"A whatty what?"

"Uh, how about a sports car worth over a million dollars."

Sheesh! "How come *you* know what that is?"

"Because I have time to live in the world instead of working sixty hours a week like you."

The doorbell rang and Shondra waved Lisa away. But her roommate hovered behind her, still eating her dinner as she watched Shondra like a movie of the week.

"Hi, Connor. Did you have trouble finding my place?"

He stepped into the foyer wearing khakis and a navy blazer with a blue-striped shirt, open at the collar to show off his tan. "Not at all."

Lisa shuffled behind her and Shondra rushed to introduce them. "Connor, this is my roommate, Lisa."

He reached out to shake her hand. "Nice to meet you, Lisa." His lady-killer smile was in full force and Lisa squeaked in return.

Shondra thought her friend was going to drop her bowl and lick Connor's face. She turned to Shondra with envy in her eyes and mouthed the words "I hate you." Then Lisa batted her eyelashes comically in Connor's direction. "You two have fun," she called over her shoulder, twisting her hips as she headed down the hallway, fanning herself.

Aside from being embarrassing, her friend's spectacle got rid of the last of Shondra's nerves. She met Connor's ice-blue gaze and the two of them cracked up laughing.

He escorted her out to his car—a stunning combination of midnight and cobalt blues—and Shondra didn't have to be an expert to know that this wasn't a car just anyone drove. Her gaze slid over the sexy, rounded curves like silk.

"Okay, now you're just showing off," she said as he opened the door for her.

Rounding the car, he slid in beside her. "Damn right. Is it working?"

"I don't know." Shondra shrugged to appear casual, taking in the earthy clay-colored leather interior. A stunning mix of chrome and black, the steering wheel and console stood out in the finely crafted luxury surrounding her. She wouldn't admit she *was* impressed. "I would think a guy like you wouldn't have to work so hard."

Connor pulled off with the attention-grabbing rev of a powerful engine. He winked at her. "No one ever *has* to work hard. But some of us don't know any other way."

As they sped out of her neighborhood, Shondra felt a little thrill bubble up inside her. She was in uncharted waters. Although she'd grown up with money—lots of it—and had always had access to nice things, she was beginning to realize that Connor was playing in a whole other league.

When she dated the average working-class man, Shondra knew where she stood. She was the one in control—often paying or going Dutch on the bills, and dictating when and where for most dates.

Tonight felt very different. Connor was every bit as smart as she was. He had more money. And he was her boss. If she wasn't careful, she was at risk of becoming Connor's plaything or worse…a novelty.

Getting involved with a powerful man was dangerous. And that fed her wild streak. The one she never indulged.

Connor must have read the expression on her face, because he looked over and said, "Relax. It's just dinner."

So she let herself relax. Determined not to overthink things any further, Shondra sank back into the seat and enjoyed the ride, as downtown Houston whizzed by her.

Twenty minutes later Connor gave his keys to the valet at a trendy restaurant she'd always wanted to try.

"Great choice. I hear the food here is top-notch," she said as they were seated at a private spot surrounded by potted palms.

"I thought you'd like it. The chef is a friend of my father's. He makes the most tender porterhouse steak you've ever had."

Shondra looked up from her menu. "A real meat and potatoes kind of guy—is that you?"

He grinned, flashing that smile that tickled her spine. "We're in Texas. What do you think?"

"I think it's not healthy to eat a lot of red meat."

"Ah, you're one of those." He winked at her.

She straightened her spine. "One of those what? Sensible people who don't plan on having open-heart surgery before the age of forty?"

Connor laughed, shaking his head. "So what are you going to order then? Please don't say a salad. You can't waste the superior skills of Chef Lerac on greenery."

Shondra folded her menu. "Actually, I think I'll have the swordfish." She eyed him with feigned deference. "If that meets with your approval, *boss*."

He looked up, not taking the bait. "I suppose it will have to do this time. But I insist you try Lerac's sweet potato mousse on the side."

Shondra agreed and when the waiter arrived, she didn't bat an eye when Connor ordered for both of them. She sipped her champagne cocktail, realizing it had been a long while since she'd been this relaxed.

Lisa had been right about one thing. She worked too hard. Sixty- to seventy-hour workweeks had been routine long before her father's passing.

Tensions had been riding high in the Braddock clan ever since her oldest brother, Malcolm, had decided to leave the family business several years ago. Shondra knew it had broken her father's heart, but she couldn't fault her brother. Malcolm had always been the type of die-hard defender of the people that never could have lasted in the political game. He couldn't understand that their father had to give away a few votes to gain ground for bigger battles.

Shondra wasn't even sure she could agree with all of her father's decisions. But she and her brother Tyson were determined not to take sides. When Malcolm walked away, their only recourse had been to focus on their own careers.

Not wanting to get lost in the melancholy that rose when she started to think about her father, she focused on Connor. He was talking about the direction he wanted to take Stewart Industries, but she scarcely heard him.

He was a truly beautiful man. His dark blond

hair, smoothed back from his face, was tucked behind each ear and hung an inch above his collar. He had a strong, rugged jaw and a sexy dimple in his right cheek. And although she was often captivated by his straight white teeth, it was only because she was avoiding the intensity of his gorgeous pale blue eyes.

Whew. How did any woman in the office get any work done? Suddenly his lips quirked into a sly smirk and he gave her a knowing look. That's when she realized her mistake.

He had stopped talking and was watching her…watch him.

Hating to feed the ego that a man that hot had to have, she struggled to save face.

"I'm sorry. I let myself get distracted there for a second. I was trying to remember if I renewed my car insurance. I know I wrote the check, but I can't remember if I mailed it."

Connor chuckled. He didn't say a word but she could tell he had noticed her ogling him.

A stinging heat rushed up her neck and bloomed in her cheeks. Picking up her water glass, she fished out an ice cube and began to suck it for a moment before crunching it between her teeth. It was a nervous habit she'd had since childhood.

Anxious to force them past this awkward moment, she began to ramble about her Mercedes and how she should replace it with a hybrid, but loathed car shopping. As she talked, she continued to play with her ice, completely unaware of its effect on her dinner companion.

Connor quickly found the shoe on the other foot as he watched Shondra tease him with her ice cubes. Only moments ago, he'd been awash in masculine pride as he watched her open appreciation of him. He was used to women finding him attractive, and it pleased him in particular to know that Shondra wasn't immune.

But his smug attitude didn't last. In her fluster, she began a seductive game of pulling ice cubes from her glass with her neatly manicured nails, sucking them gently with her perfect plum lips, then plopping them into her mouth.

It was mesmerizing and his pants were becoming uncomfortably tight. He'd had women attempt seductions in a variety of ways, but there was never any challenge in that. Shondra's unconscious act was more erotic to Connor than a thong-clad girl gyrating on a pole.

Connor watched Shondra with new appreciation. He'd found her attractive from the start. Wearing only a bit of eyeliner and lip gloss, she didn't hide her beauty under a lot of makeup. Her glossy hair was parted slightly off-center and fell in brown-black curls past her shoulders. It was the perfect frame for her heart-shaped face. She was all cheeks and dimples, with a girlishly wide smile that belied her normally serious demeanor.

He was glad she'd worn a dress tonight. It was a simple dark pink tank dress that tied behind her neck, smoothed over her ribs and flared from her hips to her knees. It left plenty of her rich, cocoa-brown skin to gleam in the candlelight, making Connor long to find out if it was as soft as it looked.

Connor knew his father wouldn't approve of his dating an SI employee. And until tonight, he'd found it easy to resist what few temptations he'd found at work. But after his flight back to Houston with Shondra, discussing business, politics and current affairs, he found himself wanting to look beyond her professional image.

Their easy flirtations were leading Connor to suspect he was in over his head. Her effect on him was more than just the thrill of breaking the rules.

The waiter appeared with their orders not a

moment too soon for Connor. It gave him something other than Shondra to focus on, and it gave her something else to do besides frustrate him with those damn ice cubes.

He sliced into his porterhouse, cooked to a perfect medium-rare. "Ah, it looks like Chef Lerac has outdone himself. How is your swordfish?"

Shondra cut into her fish with her fork and tasted it. "Mmm, it's delicious. Would you like to try some?"

"Only if you'll take a bite of this."

She shrugged. "Sure, I'm not morally opposed to eating beef. I just don't have it very often."

He held out a juicy pink cut of his steak. And instead of eating it off his fork, as he hoped, she traded utensils with him, offering him a tender slice of her swordfish.

Connor sampled what he was offered. The flavors were clean and simple, but he definitely preferred the savory spice of his steak. "It's very good—"

He lost his breath watching Shondra chew the steak with her eyes closed. "Oh my God, that practically melted in my mouth."

"Would you like another piece?"

She eyed his plate guiltily, as though she

wanted more but didn't want to ask. Without hesitation Connor cut a bigger chunk and placed it on her plate.

He'd only taken a couple more bites before he noticed that Shondra had finished what he'd given her and was eating her fish with much less enthusiasm than before.

He grinned wickedly. "Are you regretting your decision not to get the steak?"

Shondra smiled sheepishly. "Yes."

Connor's brows rose. He'd expected her to hold her pride by denying it. "An honest answer. For that you deserve a reward."

She frowned. "What do you mean?"

Connor picked up her plate and swapped it with his own.

"Oh, no!" She gasped. "I can't let you do that."

He waved her off. "Nonsense. You'd be doing me a favor. I probably eat too much red meat. After all, I'd hate to have open-heart surgery before the age of forty."

Sacrificing his meal proved to be well worth it. Despite her reluctant acceptance, she treated him to a rapturous stream of "mmms" and "ahs" that raised his temperature.

After dinner, the valet pulled his car up to the

curb. The young kid was grinning from ear to ear. "Here's your car, Mr. Stewart. That was my first time in a Bugatti. She sure is powerful."

"Yes, she is," he said, handing the kid a tip.

As he steered Shondra toward the car, she commented, "It really *is* pretty. I guess it's really fast, too?"

He typically brought the car along on first dates, because he typically dated women who knew exactly how rare and expensive a Bugatti Veyron was. Shondra, on the other hand, had only seemed mildly impressed that it was so "pretty." And, strangely enough, that pleased Connor.

He knew, for a change, that her attraction to him had nothing to do with his bank account. And despite their exchange of heated looks, he knew their rapport was based on more than the physical. Until then, he hadn't even known he was looking for more.

Shondra wanted to know if the car was fast. Connor resisted the urge to snort at the understatement. Instead he reacted on impulse, pushing the keys into her hand. "Wanna drive it?"

Handing over his car keys was something he never did. And if he was expecting her to hesitate, he was wrong.

"Hell yes!" she said, circling around to the driver's seat.

The heavy-duty engine roared to life when she put the keys in the ignition. She pulled into traffic with a jerk.

Shondra looked over at him and laughed. "Don't look so nervous. I'm a great driver. I just need a second to get used to a car with this much horsepower."

Connor gripped the door handle. "I'm not nervous," he lied. "I just want to make sure you realize this is one of the fastest-accelerating vehicles that's street legal. Take it easy."

She increased her speed, unfazed by his words. "Get a lot of traffic tickets, don't ya?"

Connor laughed. "No comment."

He busied himself cranking up his favorite hip-hop station on the satellite radio so she wouldn't see him fidgeting.

It didn't take long for Shondra to get into sync with the car and gingerly maneuver through the downtown streets. She looked over at him as the speakers started vibrating from the thundering bass. "You're not playing that for my benefit, are you?"

Connor's brow wrinkled in confusion before

he felt the back of his neck start to burn with embarrassment. She thought he was playing a rap song because she was black.

"No, not at all. This is what I normally listen to." Anxious to prove it, he dug a few CD cases out of the glove compartment. "See. Ludicrous, Chris Brown…Snoop…."

She shrugged indifferently. "Okay. Do you have any Rascal Flatts or Faith Hill?"

He grimaced. "Country music?"

She laughed. "Of course. It's my favorite."

He studied her profile. "Really? Don't you like hip-hop?"

She shook her head. "Not that much. Don't you like country?"

"Not at all."

Shondra shot him an incredulous look. "How can you be a born-and-bred Texan without liking country music?"

"Very easily. And I could ask you the same thing. Seventy percent of popular music is hip-hop. What's not to like?"

"Seventy percent? You made that up."

He shrugged. "So, it sounds true, doesn't it?"

She laughed and they agreed to compromise by switching to an 80s station. Cindy Lauper's

"Girls Just Want to Have Fun" started playing, and Shondra bounced in her seat and started singing along.

Once they drove out of town, Shondra really opened the car up.

A wild giggle burbled out of her throat and Connor was fully captivated. He laughed along with her, getting an extra rush from watching her experience the Bugatti's power for the first time.

So Shondra had a wild streak. He liked that a lot.

Shondra pulled Connor's car to a screeching halt in her driveway and turned off the engine. "That was amazing. Thanks for letting me drive."

"No problem. Once I was sure you weren't going to kill us, it was really fun. Especially watching you sing at the top of your lungs while doing one-eighty."

Shondra's eyes went wide. "I did *not* drive that fast."

"Yes, you did. But don't feel bad. In a Bugatti one-eighty is like sixty. It's such a smooth transition you don't even feel it."

She clutched a hand to her racing heart. "I'm lucky we didn't get arrested."

His wicked grin flashed. "That's the thrill of it, isn't it?"

Together they walked up her driveway, Shondra's blood still sizzling from the adrenaline rush. Connor had all the makings of a billionaire playboy. Just the type she'd carefully avoided all her life.

She was starting to wonder why. Billionaire boys had billionaire toys that were really fun to play with. But could she afford to play in Connor's sandbox?

They stopped in front of her door and Shondra looked up from finding her keys to thank him for the evening. Before she could get any words out of her mouth, he was pulling her close.

The next thing she knew, she was flattened against his chest and his soft, firm lips were on hers.

A flash of hunger shot through her in his strong, purposeful embrace. Shondra gave herself a moment to enjoy his kiss—soft and heated with just the tiniest flick of tongue—before she pulled away, breathless.

"Connor," she said when she finally regained her voice. "Thank you for dinner and a really fun evening. But as much as I'd like to continue where we just left off, I really don't think it's wise for us to get involved. After all, you're my boss."

Her throat ached a bit as she said the words, and part of her wished she could take them back as soon as she'd said them.

He eyed her with his heavy-lidded gaze for a moment, clearly trying to push through his desire to process her words.

Finally, Connor straightened his collar. "Of course, you're right. It wouldn't be wise."

They said good-night and Shondra let herself into her condo. She'd narrowly escaped temptation. As she slipped out of her shoes and padded toward her room, she admitted that Connor might not be so easy to resist in the future.

Shondra started to push open her bedroom door and stopped in her tracks. Something was bothering her.

Connor had said he agreed they shouldn't get involved, but those wicked blue eyes had been sending a different message.

Something along the lines of…*I like a challenge*.

Chapter 3

Shondra sat in her office poring over contracts until she thought her eyes would cross. As was typical with a new position, she'd had back-to-back meetings all morning, introducing herself to other department heads and making sure they were all up to speed with her agenda. That had left Shondra with only her lunch hour for research.

After an unsettling weekend, during which she'd spent too much time pushing Connor out of her mind, Shondra had shown up this morning a woman on a mission. In addition to her normal workload, Shondra's side investigation should have kept her far too occupied for lustful thoughts.

Her first order of business had been to find out how to track down the main switchboard's call list. There had to be a way to discover which extension her father had been transferred to, as well as the outgoing calls from each extension. Of course, getting what she needed on the first try would have been too much to ask. None of the employees' extensions matched with her father's phone log or the anonymous caller. But the numbers were registered to the company, so they might belong to an empty office or an old mobile phone.

Forced to take a more in-depth investigative approach, Shondra decided to search for any business dealings that tracked back to Harmon Braddock. That basically amounted to looking through files to see if her father's name came up.

A computer search of the company files revealed that a lot of what she wanted was either password protected or on coded hard drives.

Once again, she found herself butting up against a wall. It was painfully clear that security and confidentiality were a high priority within the company.

That meant she was going to have to go about finding facts the hard way. Shondra had immediate access to several contractor and client contracts so she decided to start there. Hopefully, she'd find some mention of a business relationship between Harmon Braddock and Stewart Industries.

That wouldn't clear up whether or not her father's accident had been murder, but it could turn up the name of a contact she could follow up with. It could also show that Connor's family had a legitimate connection to her father, rather than one behind closed doors. Shondra couldn't deny that she had a new vested interest in that outcome.

Glancing up at the clock, she realized she only had fifteen minutes to grab a sandwich at the corner deli before her next meeting. She was in the process of grabbing her purse when her desk phone started ringing.

She picked it up, secretly hoping it was her boss. "Shondra Braddock," she said into the receiver.

"Shawnie."

Shondra winced at her childhood nickname. No matter how often she told her brothers not to call her that anymore, the habit was so ingrained that they'd probably never change it.

"Malcolm? What's up? I was just on my way out to grab some lunch."

"What's up is exactly what I'd like to know. I'm still trying to figure out what possessed you to take a job at Stewart Industries."

Rolling her eyes, Shondra told her brother to hold on while she closed her office door. She was located only a few feet away from the quadrant of cubicles where the secretaries sat. If gossip traveled through this office the way it had in her previous ones, all of her business would be the late-breaking news within the hour.

Returning to her desk, Shondra resigned herself to missing lunch. Appeasing her oldest brother could take a while. He saw himself as the family protector, now more than ever.

"Okay, I'm back. And as for my new job, I've already spoken to Tyson about this. I thought he'd filled you in."

"I spoke to him, but I'm interested in hearing it from you. What exactly do you hope to accomplish?"

"Well, I'm their new CCO, so I'm in the process of designing new internal controls for—"

"Stop it. You know what I'm talking about."

Wincing, Shondra could scarcely believe this was the more laid-back version of her oldest brother. He'd mellowed quite a bit since he'd begun dating Gloria Kingsley.

Just not quite enough to stop checking up on her as though she were still twelve instead of twenty-eight.

"You and Tyson wanted to know what Dad had to do with SI. Now I'm in the perfect position to find out."

"Don't you think taking a job there is a bit rash? Why didn't you discuss it with us before you took such a prominent position within the company?"

Shondra stared out her window, wishing she could climb out of it. "Because everything moved so fast. And because I don't need your permission to change jobs."

"Shawnie, you have no idea where this could lead. What if someone working there *was* involved with Dad's death? Don't you think the Braddock name will stand out? It's entirely possible that you're putting yourself at risk."

"Don't worry, Malcolm. I'm an expert at risk management." She'd hoped to lighten the mood, but her brother wasn't having any of it.

"Don't get cute. I'm just trying to make sure you've thought this through and that you're being cautious."

Shondra had taken into consideration that if someone at SI had been involved with her father's death, her family name could put her in danger, as well. But she felt that was a chance she had to take.

To her way of thinking, it was much more significant that the anonymous warning had come from SI. She hoped that her presence would encourage that person to make contact again with more information.

"What you *should* be asking—" she was hoping to rush through the rest of this conversation "—is if I've found anything."

There was a long pause on the other end of the line, as though Malcolm was trying to decide whether or not to encourage her. "Did you find anything?" he asked with obvious reluctance.

"I spent a good bit of time looking through contracts today. I still have more to do, but I'm getting the feeling that if Dad had dealings with someone here, it wasn't related to oil."

Malcolm blew out is breath. "That's what I was afraid of."

Shondra finally got off the phone five minutes before her next meeting. Her stomach was grumbling loudly, which was the last thing she needed before tying herself up in a conference room for a couple of hours.

She knew the fifth floor had a snack machine. At least she could suck down a few chips and quiet her stomach. She was in the process of deciding between corn chips and pretzels when she heard someone come up behind her.

"A snack-machine lunch? I thought you were some kind of health nut."

The back of her neck tingled as she turned to face Connor. "It wasn't my first choice, but it's been a busy day. At this point, it's either junk food or office supplies."

Connor shook his head. "I've tasted the pencils. I can't recommend them."

Shondra laughed, feeling nervous now that she knew what his lips tasted like. And it was hard not to focus on those lips right now. He looked great today in his dark gray suit.

Feeling her skin heat, she realized she was staring. Grateful for something to do, she spun away, thrust her coins into the machine and punched J5 for the pretzels.

And, of course, they got stuck on the coil. She slammed her palm into the glass to no avail.

"Here, let me help you with that."

Shondra started to move aside, but Connor had already trapped her against the machine with his body. He was now close enough for her to smell the clean, fresh scent of his soap. Her heartbeat sped up, and she hoped she wasn't perspiring, because she was feeling really hot.

Gripping both sides of the vending machine, Connor gave it a vigorous shake, bringing his body into contact with hers. Shondra sucked in her breath. The whole exercise took less than thirty seconds but she felt as if time had been moving in slow motion.

Without stepping back from her, he reached down and plucked the bag from the tray. "Here you go," he said, placing it into her hand while his other hand slipped down to rest on her waist.

Shondra turned in his arms and for a split second she was tempted to let him kiss her.

But her sanity returned as she realized they were standing in the alcove of a busy corridor. Someone could pass through at any moment.

Face flaming, Shondra eased out from between

Connor and the machine. "Thanks," she squeaked, and rushed down the hall to the elevator.

Connor laughed to himself as he watched Shondra run off. Good. She had it as bad as he did. If he didn't have a meeting himself, he'd go after her and really make her squirm.

She'd been on his mind all weekend. They had agreed not to get involved, but Connor didn't think she wanted that any more than he did. And if they both wanted it, why should they both suffer?

Connor walked into his office whistling. He loved the chase. After gathering his projections for the new oil well, he headed to the conference room to review the figures with his stockholders.

Pushing through the double doors, he stopped short. His father was sitting in his position at the head of the table. He ignored the rows of eyes on him as he stood over his father.

"There must have been a miscommunication, Carl." He couldn't stand calling the man "Dad" in front of his colleagues. "I thought I was going to be running this meeting."

Carl Stewart straightened in his seat. "You are, Connor. I'm just sitting in."

Trying to hide the radical spike in his blood pressure, Connor settled himself in the seat next to his father's.

The sixty-six-year-old man resisted aging at every cost. As a result, his dirty-blond dye job and string of young companions fooled many into thinking that Carl Stewart was a modern man. But the reality was that he was still a traditionalist who clung to the old ways like a life preserver.

He always did this. He was supposed to be phasing out of the company, making room for Connor to take the helm as CEO. But, typical of their relationship, his father just couldn't let go.

As long as he attended all the meetings and held tight to the company reins, Carl could ensure that things continued to be done the way they always had been. That meant more vetoes for Connor's ideas.

As long as his father showed up to work in the morning, the employees would continue to defer to him. How could they respect Connor as their boss if his father continued to act as if he needed to monitor his son at every turn? That's why Connor spent as much time as he could on oil rigs. Out there, the employees respected *him*.

With gritted teeth, Connor barreled his way

through the meeting despite his father's constant interjections, anecdotes and questions. He wanted nothing more than to confront the elder Stewart about the situation, but it wasn't the time to make waves.

His father would never retire if Connor couldn't convince him that he could run the business with a cool head. That included finessing the old man.

If he bided his time, everything would go as planned. Carl Stewart would retire, and Connor would finally be free to run the company on his own.

At least that's what he told himself. He could play his father's game for a few more months, Connor reassured himself as he stalked past his executive assistant into his office.

But not without a little distraction for himself, he thought, picking up his phone to dial Shondra's extension.

By Thursday afternoon Shondra was beginning to wonder if she'd gotten herself in over her head.

It took a lot of energy to rebuff Connor's flirtations and do her work. No less than once a day she received phone calls, voice mails or e-mails, and although she found these to be the brightest spots in her day, they were distracting enough that she had to stay late in the evenings to keep ahead of her workload.

As if that wasn't enough, anytime she found a spare moment she tried to do a little investigating.

Tomorrow she'd be boarding a plane to South America to tour another SI facility and look into their compliance issues. She wanted to make some progress today because she wouldn't be back in the office until Tuesday.

For all the documents and files she had to sort through, she was coming up with exactly nothing. Worse yet, she was starting to count on Connor's distractions to get her through the day.

He often called with silly questions to get her caught up in mindless banter. He was quick with words and their verbal sparring was more fun than it should have been.

And when he wasn't calling, he managed to "run into her" in the break room, the elevator or even the deli where she liked to go for lunch.

The only place they hadn't crossed paths—

There was a knock on her door.

—was her office.

"Come in."

Connor slipped through the door and immediately came to tower over her desk.

"What are you doing here?" Shondra's spine snapped straight. He'd caught her off guard. At that moment her desk was piled with files she'd snuck from a fifth-floor filing cabinet that she had no business accessing.

She wouldn't be able to explain herself if Connor realized she was snooping around where she didn't belong.

He circled her desk until he could lean against the edge, looming in her personal space. "What am I doing here? Is that any way to greet your boss?"

Shondra pushed back until her desk chair hit the wall at her back. She needed air and a means to distract him. The last thing she needed was for him to focus on the contents of her desk.

Her heart was racing in her chest. She hoped she didn't look nervous. Fortunately she suspected that if she did, Connor would thank his masculine charms before he looked elsewhere for an explanation.

"Technically, your father's my boss." Shondra noted a pained look on his face that was gone before she could analyze it. "Is there anything I can do for you, sir?" she said with mock sweetness.

Shondra held her breath as he turned and looked over her desk. He grabbed a pencil out of her organizer and pretended to inspect it. "I just dropped by to make sure you weren't snacking between meals."

Shondra snatched the pencil away. "Thanks, but I haven't had to resort to eating the office supplies yet."

Connor leaned closer. "I'm glad to hear it. But I've noticed that you work through lunch quite a bit. That's not healthy. I take the proper nourishment of my employees very seriously, so I'm going to take you to lunch today."

Shondra shook her head. That was all she needed. So far, no one had noticed their little interactions around the office, but if they went to lunch, people would start to notice. She couldn't stand the idea of being the object of office gossip and she told him as much.

"Besides," she added, "I'm actually having lunch with Sarah today. So you don't have to worry about me after all."

Connor frowned. "You're having lunch with my executive assistant? Why?"

"Because she's nice and we hit it off." Which was true; they'd run into each other a few times in the break room and had a lot in common. But she also thought a lunch date would give her a chance to find out if the woman had ever received any calls from her father.

"Now, if you'll excuse me," she said, standing and steering him toward the door, "I've got a few more things to get done before Sarah and I leave."

Connor allowed himself to be ushered out and Shondra almost burst into laughter at his slightly confused expression.

Shondra took Sarah to a Mexican restaurant that was within walking distance of the office.

"Thanks for inviting me to lunch," the woman said, smiling. She appeared to be in her mid-thirties, was of average height and build and wore her brown hair in a short bob. "Usually the executives at SI like to treat the administrative staff as if they're invisible."

Shondra frowned. "That's terrible."

Sarah shrugged. "No, it's just typical."

"I have to say I think the snobbery works both ways. The administrative assistants on my floor barely speak to me, unless we're discussing work."

"They're probably afraid of you. The last CCO in that office was a real piece of work. Kind of obsessive-compulsive. He kept those girls on their toes." Sarah opened up the menu and studied the beverage list. "I wish I didn't have to go back to the office. This place makes the best margaritas."

The two of them made small talk until their orders arrived, then Shondra decided it was time to ease into her questions.

To get the ball rolling, Shondra realized she was going to have to confide in Sarah that her father had died in a car accident over a month ago. One of the best things about working for a new company was not having everyone watching her or treating her as though she were fragile.

It was nice to walk down the halls of SI without having everyone she passed asking if she was okay. Of course she wasn't okay. In fact, she counted on the times she could escape her grief by getting lost in her work. If she talked to Sarah about her father, she risked losing her privacy once again.

Her face must have been showing her turmoil because Sarah leaned over. "Are you okay?"

Shondra took a deep breath and dove in. "I'm sorry if I look like I zoned out there for a moment. My father died not too long ago."

Sarah immediately reached out to grab her hand. "I'm so sorry to hear that. Had he been ill?"

"No, it was a car accident. Very sudden."

Sarah wrinkled her brow. "Really? I'm so sorry."

"You never heard the name Harmon Braddock? I thought he knew someone at Stewart Industries."

Sarah shrugged. "No, I don't think I've heard of him. But you know, if you ever need anything, you can come to me. My father died five years ago, and sometimes it still feels like it happened just yesterday. Losing a parent is tough."

Shondra felt her grief welling up and she pushed it back down. She couldn't get anything done if she let herself sink into depression. Compartmentalizing her feelings was her best coping mechanism. That meant whenever she felt the pain surface, she put it in a box and closed the lid on it. Thankfully, that had been working so far.

One thing was for certain. She couldn't find any evidence that her father had had a business connection with SI. The only thing left to do was to check out the phone logs for SI.

Unfortunately no one was going to just hand those over to her if she asked. And there weren't many ways to access it on her own without arousing suspicion.

After sharing such a personal moment with Sarah, the two of them were able to relax and chat like old friends. And befriending Connor's assistant had another unexpected benefit. Gossip.

"You'd never know it if you saw the backseat of Connor's BMW—he gave me a ride home once—but he's got the slightest touch of OCD when it comes to his desk. Pencils here, pens there, files stacked to the left. He claims he can't think straight if his desk isn't organized."

"Whew, that sounds tough."

"He knows what he wants, that's for sure. But he's great to work for. He makes his own coffee and orders his own lunch. Most executives I've worked for barely know how to use the high-powered computers that sit on their desks, but Connor is very savvy. In fact, he has a lot of ideas to update the technology at SI, if his father ever retires."

Shondra sat up straight. "What do you mean?"

"Carl Stewart has been dangling the title of CEO over Connor for the last year and a half. It's his way of getting his son to jump through hoops. But whenever the time comes for the old man to step down, he finds some reason to linger on. Part of me thinks he has no intention of quitting. He probably plans to die sitting up in that massive leather throne of his."

Sarah must have realized she'd let her bitterness show because she darted a startled look to Shondra, gauging her reaction.

Shondra smiled. "Connor's lucky to have such a loyal assistant."

Relaxing again, Sarah laughed. "No, I'm the lucky one. Have you seen him? I love the days he goes to the gym after work because he puts on these tight T-shirts and shorts. Wow!"

Shondra laughed, surprised at the sudden prick of jealousy she felt. "I'm sure all the women in the office are googly-eyed over him."

"You're not kidding. In fact, the only complaint I have about working for Connor is having to fight off the women. Especially accounting. Those girls take turns running up to get his personal approval on things they could send through interoffice mail."

She tried to keep her tone neutral as she asked, "Does he ever date any of them?"

Sarah snorted. "Are you kidding? There's no way. Even if he wanted to, he wouldn't. An office romance gone wrong, potential sexual harassment suits—that would be all Carl would need to take the CEO title off the table completely."

Shondra didn't know what to make of Sarah's words. But they made her inexplicably happy.

The SI car service picked Shondra up at her condo just after 6:00 a.m. Friday morning. She'd been told by the accounting department that the driver would bring her airline tickets.

She was shocked for the second time when she was taken to an airfield where the company jet was waiting. Shaking her head, she boarded the plane. If they kept this up, she was going to get spoiled.

Just as before, she entered the cabin and found Connor Stewart waiting for her.

"Let me guess," she said, shaking her head. "You've got business in South America, too, and you thought we should fly together."

Connor stood and brought her a glass of mimosa. "Nope. South America is out. We're going to Monte Carlo for a long weekend."

Chapter 4

Shondra lowered herself onto the sofa, frowning with confusion. "Monte Carlo? I don't understand. I'm supposed to be in Venezuela by this evening."

Connor sat beside her. "Don't worry about that. That trip's been canceled. Now you're free to enjoy a long weekend with me."

She took a sip of the mimosa he'd thrust into her hand, trying to process the situation. Should she feel piqued at his presumptuousness? Her family always made plans for her without consulting her. It was a behavior she didn't want to encourage in someone else.

"Canceled? That doesn't make any sense. Your father hired me specifically to handle trips like Venezuela." Her words came out more sharply than she'd intended, but her temper was rising.

"Yes, but he didn't anticipate your being so good at your job. Because of all the new Internet protocols you've established in the last week, we could update the compliance issues for the Venezuela site online."

"Oh," she said blankly. A mixture of pride and confusion washed over her. So now she was supposed to take an impromptu vacation?

Of course, another way to look at it was that instead of a long weekend of work, she was going to Monte Carlo, one of the most glamourous cities in the world.

She felt a thrill of anticipation rise inside her.

"Wait a minute," she said, sitting up straight. "If you've taken care of Venezuela, then this trip isn't business, it's pleasure. Correct?"

"That's right," he said, looking as sinful as the devil himself.

"I thought we agreed to keep things strictly business between us."

"I think we can both agree that hasn't been working out too well. But if you don't want to be *here*…with *me*…right *now,* then say the word and I'll have the pilot turn back to Houston."

Shondra chewed on her lower lip. She wasn't stupid. Nothing she could plan would be better than what lay ahead for them. And the truth was, there wasn't anywhere she'd rather be—or anyone she'd rather be with.

"No, I want to go with you. I'm just not used to this kind of thing."

For the men she usually got involved with, spontaneous meant showing up at noon for a quicky. She wasn't sure how to handle this level of romantic showmanship.

"It's okay if you're caught off guard," Connor said. "Life is more exciting when you don't know what will happen next."

Shondra grinned. This was living, wasn't it? She knew her family wouldn't approve, but that made the moment all the more exciting. She never allowed herself to do anything truly rebellious.

Instead she always did what was best for her family image. After twenty-eight years of obedience, hadn't she earned the right to a little fun? Shondra was on a private jet headed to Monte Carlo, where no one would know her. Why not let her hair down a little?

Shondra finished her mimosa and held her glass out. "More, please."

Connor laughed, grabbing a pitcher to fill her glass. "Now that's the spirit. And, just so you know, it's just the two of us—and the pilot, of course—so feel free to make yourself comfortable."

Shondra felt her heartbeat pick up. Suddenly she was fully aware of what going away for the weekend with Connor could mean. No more fantasies. No more sleepless nights. This was the real thing. He was flesh and blood and only an arm's length away.

Her cheeks flushed at the possibilities. Hoping he couldn't guess her thoughts, Shondra racked her brain for something to say. Could he tell that she was suddenly very nervous?

She gulped at her mimosa and smoothed her hair from her face. "I've never been to Monte Carlo."

Connor smiled. "You're going to love it."

"Monte Carlo's in Monaco. They speak French there, right?"

"Oui, mademoiselle, et le Français est la langue de l'amour," he said, taking their glasses and setting them aside.

She looked at him in surprise. It wasn't hard to guess what that meant. "Oh, you speak French?"

"Yes. Actually, I'm fluent in four languages."

Shondra leaned in, impressed. "Really? Which ones?"

"English, French, Spanish and German."

"Wow." The more Shondra learned about Connor, the more she liked him. He was living proof that looks were deceiving. On the outside he appeared to be a wealthy playboy with nothing to offer but his family name. But in reality, he was clever and down to earth.

"What about you? Do you speak any other languages?"

She laughed. "I'm a little rusty on my high school Spanish. And, of course, I speak excellent legalese." She laughed.

"Okay, how about I give you a little refresher course." Connor leaned over and touched Shondra's head. *"Cabeza."*

"Cabeza," Shondra repeated.

His fingertip trailed down to her nose. *"Nariz."*

"Nariz," she whispered, feeling her mouth go dry at his nearness.

He touched his lips gently to hers, then whispered, *"Labios,"* against them.

Shondra parted her lips to repeat the word and Connor's tongued slipped into her mouth. At that point all words—even the English ones—evaporated from her head.

His lips were stronger and firmer than in their first kiss, as though his need was finally unrestrained.

Shondra felt a moment of panic. If she allowed the kiss to really take off, there would be no turning back. Connor's lips softened as he explored her mouth. And Shondra gave in.

Her head was already in the clouds. Her heart could be destined for a crash landing, but she'd have to risk it.

He reached over and pulled her across his lap. Lowering his mouth to her neck, he nibbled at the soft, sensitive skin there and hurried to push her blazer off her shoulders.

Shondra helped by shrugging out of it, and Connor tossed it on the seat behind her. As his fingers found the buttons on the back of her blouse, Shondra lifted up so she could straddle him.

Now they were face-to-face. His eyes were hooded with desire and his lips were slightly parted. He wanted her. Shondra felt a rush of power. This beautiful man wanted her. Right here. Right now.

Behind his head was a long window and

Shondra could see nothing but clouds surrounding them. They were in the air, and she was flying high on the moment. Shondra reached up and ran her fingers through his blond waves. It was a new experience to be able to do that. She took a moment to enjoy the sensation of the strands threading her fingers. Finally she brushed his hair back from his face and let her nails gently rake his scalp.

Connor moaned, gripping her tighter around the waist and rocking against her. She framed his face with her hands and pressed her mouth to his, pouring all of her desires into the kiss. Her desire to break the rules… To feel his body flattened under hers… To make love to a gorgeous man who wanted her.

"Oh my God," Connor gasped. He pulled back just enough to pull her shirt off.

If Shondra had known where this weekend was really headed, she would have packed sexier lingerie. Instead she was wearing a simple gray cotton bra and panty set, trimmed in pink piping.

Fortunately, Connor barely noticed as he made short work of her bra hook and slipped it off her shoulders. Shondra's breath left her in a rush as he pressed his lips to the side of her neck. His lips made a delicate trail over her collarbone, to the indentation of her throat and down to her cleavage.

His broad hands glided up her back, pushing her breasts up into the air. Connor's tongue gently circled one nipple, then the other, giving equal time to both as his mouth sucked and nipped at her breasts.

Shondra began to squirm as she felt her impatience growing. Pushing Connor back against the sofa, she started pulling at the buttons on his shirt. He helped her remove it, and Shondra felt a sense of victory as she gazed upon the golden expanse of masculine beauty before her.

Her hands smoothed over his chest, letting her fingertips find every muscular ridge on the surface. Then she leaned forward and treated him to the same exquisite torture he'd given her nipples. She flicked the tiny male peaks with her tongue and Connor wriggled, pulling back. "That tickles."

Shondra laughed, but took the opportunity to get to her feet. She felt warm and the need to be free from constriction. As she pulled off her slacks, Connor did the same, revealing a form-fitting pair of navy-blue boxer-briefs.

As Shondra admired them, they disappeared before her eyes.

"Now it's your turn," he said, nodding to the gray cotton boy-shorts that shielded the last of her modesty.

Unable to take her eyes off his trim, muscular body, Shondra stepped out of her panties and dropped them in the chair with the rest of her clothes.

Connor's Adam's apple bobbed as he swallowed hard. His pale eyes were intense and locked on her. The wicked, smug grin he usually wore was gone. He held his arms out to her. She stepped forward into them.

He cupped the back of her neck and kissed her hungrily. His engine roared to life and they were soaring at full speed. Connor lowered himself onto the sofa and pulled Shondra down on top of him. His hands were everywhere, and Shondra thrilled at the feel of their bodies meshed together.

"I neglected to finish my Spanish lesson," Connor said, stroking her shoulder. "This is your *hombro*."

He rubbed his hand over her back. "And your *parte posteriora*."

Shondra sat up. "My turn." She ran her hand down his torso, past his navel and lower. "I remember the word for this," she said, taking him in her hand.

He choked. "You learned that word in Spanish class?"

She laughed. "No, I learned that word from a couple of girls in my gym class. They taught me how to swear in Spanish. And of course, they threw in a few other interesting phrases."

Shondra started repeating the phrases she remembered how to say, and Connor became fully aroused.

He leaned up to kiss her, and his fingers slipped between their bodies to make her ready for him.

Shondra jerked up. "Do you have condoms?"

Connor winced, pointing to a bag on the other side of the sofa. "Side pocket."

Jumping up, she dashed to the bag and rummaged in the side pocket. She immediately pulled out a jumbo box. "Feeling confident, weren't you?"

Connor's grin was sheepish. "Come back here. Quick."

Shondra dug into the box and took out a packet. Then she climbed back up over Connor's body, gingerly avoiding the large obstacle in her path.

He pulled her down to kiss her and Shondra pressed the packet into his hands.

Connor put on the condom and raised her hips to slowly lower her onto him.

Shondra worked her hips and relished the mounting excitement of the moment. She looked out the window and felt as though she were riding the clouds.

Connor helped guide her movements with one hand on her hip, while the other fondled her breast. He murmured words of encouragement as she raised and lowered in an escalating rhythm.

Shondra threw back her head and flew to her peak. Crying out his pleasure, Connor followed.

She collapsed on Connor's chest. After several minutes he got up to visit the lavatory. He returned with an afghan. He climbed back onto the sofa and placed a pillow behind his head. Shondra pillowed her head on his chest, once again, and Connor settled the blanket over their bodies.

Exhausted from the early hour, two mimosas and their spontaneous workout, Shondra and Connor slept for several hours. She woke up snuggled on his chest. He had one leg dragging the floor and the other leg curled around hers.

She lifted her head and became immediately disoriented when she saw nothing but ocean below them through the window. Connor groaned and eased himself into a sitting position.

"I'm starving. How about you?"

"Uh, yeah, I'm hungry," Shondra said, moving aside so he could get up. She smoothed her hair with both hands, then reached for the blanket to cover herself.

Connor pulled on his boxer-briefs. "I'll be right back with some lunch." He disappeared behind a curtain at the back of the plane.

Shondra grabbed her underwear and quickly dressed. She was just reaching for her blouse and slacks when Connor emerged from the curtain carrying a tray.

"Uh-uh-uh, this flight is underwear or less from here on out."

Shondra gave him a puzzled look, but returned to sit as Connor strutted up the aisle. She had to admit, that plan had its perks.

He placed the tray on the table between two large leather seats across from the sofa. "For lunch today, I'll be serving a lobster salad, a cold cucumber soup with Parmesan toast, and chocolate mousse with fresh raspberries for dessert."

Shondra rubbed her hands together. "That sounds delicious. Dare I ask if you made it yourself?"

Connor laughed. "Not this time. But I *can* cook."

She scoffed. "And by cooking do you mean throwing steaks on the grill?"

"No, I *can* cook. I didn't study at the Cordon Bleu or anything, but I can hold my own in the kitchen. I'll cook for you sometime."

Shondra's heart hammered in her chest. He'd cook for her sometime? Future plans implied the potential for a long-term relationship.

She shook her head. She couldn't think about what would happen beyond the weekend. There were too many complications, and thinking about them would just put a damper on the live-in-the moment spirit she was trying to adopt at least temporarily.

She joined him at the table and Connor asked, "What about you? Do you cook?"

"Not even a little bit."

"Ah, not the domestic type?"

"I'm afraid not. But if you want to know about

the latest legal codes and government regulations, I'm your girl. I can also assemble a computer from the inside out and beat both my brothers at basketball. Sometimes. And I know all the words to 'Wide Open Spaces' by the Dixie Chicks."

Connor shook his head. "So you really weren't kidding about that country music stuff, were you?"

"No, I wasn't. And you'd do well to listen to more of it. How can you call yourself a true Texan?"

"Easily. And what about you? Don't you think you're closing off a huge part of your own culture by not being more in tune with hip-hop music?"

Shondra shrugged indifferently.

"I bet you don't even know what this means— *the po-pos tried to beef, but I got 'em with my eight plus one.*"

She burst out laughing. Even though Connor had done his best to say it with the proper inflection, including hand gestures, the words sounded hilarious coming out of his mouth.

But he was right. She wasn't quite sure what that meant. Kicking up her twang, she replied, "And I bet you don't know what this means— *he's a real curly wolf when he bends an elbow.*"

His brow furrowed as he racked his brain, clearly trying to prove her wrong. "Fine, you got me. We have an opportunity to enrich our cultures here. Why don't I teach you hip-hop slang and you can teach me cowboy slang?"

Shondra paused, shaking her head at the concept. "Wow, that's ironic."

He laughed. "I think we both owe it to our people to fit our assigned stereotypes better."

She laughed with him. "Okay, you've got a deal. 'He's a real curly wolf when he bends an elbow' means he's a tough guy when he has a drink. What does yours mean?"

"The police tried to start trouble but I shot them with my 9-millimeter."

Shondra shook her head, laughing. "I'll file that away for my next meeting with the board."

Connor finished his salad and laughed. "See *now* we're getting to know each other."

Shondra nodded, taking a sip of her cucumber soup. "Yes, I now know that you consider yourself a good cook and speak four languages, not including hip-hop, fluently."

"Yes, but there's still a lot I'd like to know about you. Tell me about your family."

Shondra bit her lip. She didn't want to talk

about her family. Thinking about her brothers reminded her of the real reason she was working for Stewart Industries. And she didn't want to think about that while she was with Connor.

She tried to answer his question without too much detail. "I have two brothers. They're very protective of me because I'm the baby. That's all, really. Nothing much to tell. What about—"

"Really? What about your parents?"

Shondra put down her fork. Her appetite was gone. She shook her head. "I—I—"

Connor reached across and touched her hand. "Shondra, Sarah told me that your father passed away recently."

Shondra gasped and before she realized what was happening, tears that had welled in her eyes started streaming down her cheeks.

Chapter 5

Connor swore viciously under his breath as he watched Shondra sob into her hands, her shoulders shaking. What the hell had he been thinking? In a matter of seconds he'd caused her to go from goofy laughter to heart-wrenching grief. "Oh, honey, I'm sorry."

Rushing around the table, he pulled her up into his arms. Clutching her tightly, he whispered softly into the top of her head. "I'm so sorry. It's okay. Just let it out."

When her sobs finally subsided, Connor handed her a wad of napkins to dry her face.

Then he guided her to the sofa, scooting her onto his lap.

He could feel her shyness. She kept her cheek pressed against his chest as he stroked her back to soothe her. Finally she seemed to muster the courage to meet his eyes. "I'm sorry about that. I feel like such a fool."

He brushed a bit of lint from the wadded napkins off her face. "Don't be silly. This is all my fault. I feel like an insensitive jerk."

She took a deep, shaky breath. "No, you couldn't have known that would happen. I didn't even know. I thought I was holding up so well."

"I *should* have known." Connor squeezed her shoulder. "My mother died ten years ago. I remember how randomly the grief can hit you. For me, months would pass then I'd hear a song she used to love or see a woman carrying a handbag like the one she had…and I'd lose it."

She looked up at him wide-eyed. He'd never seen her so vulnerable. Shondra's meticulous record-keeping and affinity for schedules down to the minute showed her as a woman of order and control. Connor knew she hated having a witness to her breakdown.

He hoped knowing that he'd experienced a similar loss would ease her discomfort.

She reached up and touched his face. "I'm sorry about your mother. Was she sick?"

"Breast cancer."

Shondra gave a somber nod of sympathy. He'd once been well acquainted with that nod. Again he kicked himself for raising the subject of her father's death so cavalierly.

Connor stroked her hair and she rested her face against his chest again. He felt new tears on his skin. "You've been holding a lot in, haven't you? I want you to know whatever you feel is okay. You don't have to run from it."

She sat up straight. "No. I grieved. I cried. For almost a solid month it seems, I cried."

"And since then?"

Shondra exhaled. "I can't spend the rest of my life crying. I have work to do. I have family obligations. I need to find out if my—" She turned away. "I'm just rambling. I don't know what I feel."

Connor didn't question her. He knew that feeling. At least his own version of it. "When you think you've wallowed in the pain enough, you start shutting down. You stop dealing with it. Believe me, I know."

She looked at him, her eyes encouraging him to continue.

"For me, it was 'acting out.' That's what the shrink my dad sent me to called it. I spent a lot of money. I stayed out all night and got into whatever trouble I could think of."

Connor watched her face and when she didn't seem to be shocked, he continued. "Knowing my mother was sick didn't make her death any easier."

He felt a knot forming in his throat. Even after ten years the pain was still there, waiting to resurface. "My father was convinced that he could buy his way out of anything, even my mother's breast cancer. She had the best doctors in the country. Expensive and painful treatments. Every experimental drug that came onto the market. He flew her from one clinic to another whenever he heard some new method was being attempted.

"My mother became exhausted. None of it was working. She had to beg him to finally let go. To let her die."

Shondra hugged him tight. "I know that was awful for you."

He nodded, lost in the memory.

Shondra took a deep breath. "My father died in a car crash. His death was very sudden. He'd always been very healthy—he took care of himself. I had this delusion that he was made of steel. Sometimes I still can't process that he's gone."

Shondra shivered from an invisible chill and Connor wrapped his arms around her and pulled her closer.

"Even at the funeral. I looked in the casket and I kept thinking, That's not him. That isn't my father."

Connor nodded, rocking her very gently, and Shondra wrapped both her arms around his waist. She squeezed him back.

They stayed that way for several moments, silently grieving for their parents.

As he held her, Connor was suddenly struck by the intimacy they'd just shared. Not more than an hour earlier, on that very sofa, they'd shared their bodies. But that physical intimacy had not prepared him for this new kind of intimacy. At thirty-three, there were few, if any, women with whom he'd shared such closeness.

He felt an instant of panic. Was he ready for this?

When he'd planned this weekend, part of him thought he was doing the noble thing. They'd both work better if they gave in to their feelings. Now he was starting to think they could really have something.

Shondra was the first to pull back. She turned in his arms and met his eyes. "Thank you. I'd thought the grieving was over. Clearly, I was naive. If you keep storing your emotions on a shelf, eventually the shelf breaks."

He smiled, feeling a rush of tenderness for Shondra. "I'm glad I was here when it happened. Lean on me. Anytime."

Shondra smiled back. They sat there for a moment, just grinning at each other like fools. Then she leaned forward and pressed her lips against his. It was a soft kiss, not the least bit sexual. More like a silent thank-you for understanding what she'd needed.

Connor started to shift so she could slide off his lap, but suddenly she turned, straddling his hips with her knees.

She opened her mouth, changing the kiss. He felt her tongue gently flicking at his lower lip. He parted his lips, feeling a rush of blood going straight to his core.

Connor tried to pull back. He didn't want to rush her. They'd just shared an emotional moment.

But she pressed her body into his. Shondra seemed to need something else from him.

He wrapped his arms around her, letting her find what she needed. And as she let her soft full lips trail over his face, he realized he needed something, too.

Connor let her touch and explore him for as long as he could stand. Then he lifted her, her legs still gripping his waist, and pushed her back onto the sofa.

Shondra was so beautiful. Her dark brown eyes were still glittery from her recent cry. Her lips were plump from his kisses. And her skin…

He loved her smooth dark skin. He watched his hands stroke down her body, enjoying the contrast of his tanned hands on her brown velvet thighs.

He groaned, bowing his head to kiss her bellybutton. Connor had wanted to enjoy the foreplay, but it was becoming clear that he wasn't going to last that long.

Removing their underwear, he quickly entered her. She was warm and tight, and as he buried his face in her neck, she was all there was for him.

Their union was fueled by an urgency born of pent-up emotion. It was a physical workout as

Connor used the strength of his arms to move against her body.

Shondra released herself with a loud, shouting cry that spurred his own release in an almost violent rush. They collapsed against each other, exhausted, mentally and physically spent.

When they finally recovered from their second round of lovemaking, Shondra insisted on putting on her clothes.

Connor lay stretched out on the sofa, naked, watching her dress. "Stop it. I thought we had a deal."

Shondra pulled on her slacks. "Sitting around in our underwear is just too dangerous."

"Dangerous for whom?"

"Dangerous for me. I need a break." She leaned over one of the seats and looked out the window. "How long is this flight, anyway?"

"Uh, I guess we've been in the air for five, almost six hours, so we have about six more to go."

Shondra slid into a seated position as Connor got up and started dressing himself. "Six more hours? Is there an in-flight movie or something?"

Connor buttoned his shirt. "I had plenty of

ideas about how we could pass our time on this flight, but they all included nudity."

She looked at him askance. "I'm sorry, but I am *not* a machine."

He laughed. "Now you're a member of the mile-high club."

Shondra perked up. "Hey, that's true. That's one little adventure I wasn't expecting to have."

Connor sat across from her. "I aim to please."

Shondra felt her face heating. He certainly did please. But she was feeling a little overwhelmed by the situation. Their relationship was rushing forward like a conveyer belt out of control. Shondra didn't know how to get off, or if she wanted to.

And she was still a bit embarrassed about her spontaneous crying jag. It had forced them into an intimate space she wasn't sure either of them was prepared for. She didn't know Connor's expectations, but she couldn't assume they went beyond having fun.

Having expectations of any kind in a relationship fraught with so many obstacles was just a setup for disappointment. But Shondra felt tears welling in her eyes yet again when she thought about how tenderly he'd treated her when she'd broken down.

Having sex afterward had only tightened the bond she was feeling. Shondra had given in to this weekend thinking she could live in the moment. Now she had no idea where she stood with Connor, or her own feelings anymore.

Pushing aside her thoughts, she tried to focus on the weekend ahead. "So what's the plan for Monte Carlo? What are we going to do…? Where are we going to stay?"

Connor leaned forward as if to tell her a secret, whispering, "There is no plan." Then in his normal voice, he said, "That's the point. Haven't you ever just decided to run off on a whim? No reservations."

"No," Shondra said, becoming alarmed. "I'm a fan of reservations. I can always get what I want when I plan ahead. You have to settle for what's left when you do things at the last minute."

Connor laughed. "Well, this weekend, you're trying it my way. Completely spontaneous. Let's just see what happens."

That concept felt unnatural—wrong, in fact. But underneath the waves of discomfort at not being in control was an unexpected thrill—anticipation. There wasn't enough of that in her life

For the rest of the trip they discussed nonsense. Shondra suspected Connor needed to keep it light as much as she did. They talked about random little things from their favorite brands of toothpaste to their surprisingly similar political beliefs. They watched a movie on DVD and had an early dinner of London broil and whipped potatoes.

When the plane finally landed just after dusk that evening, Shondra felt like she was stepping out of her own private cocoon into a whole new world.

It seemed the instant they set foot onto the tarmac in Nice, France, Connor's cell phone started ringing.

"Uh-oh—" Shondra joked. "The outside world has found us."

Connor didn't respond. He just gazed at the number in the little window with a puzzled expression before snapping it shut.

"Aren't you going to answer that?"

He turned off the phone and tucked it into his shirt pocket. "It's business. This weekend is all about pleasure."

After a quick stop through customs, they were off again.

A helicopter was waiting to take them to

Monaco, where a Town Car met them when they landed. When the driver pulled up in front of the Hotel Metropole Monaco, Shondra turned and punched Connor in the arm.

"Ouch. What was that for?"

"You said we were being spontaneous. The helicopter, the car—you must have arranged those in advance. And I suspect you have a reservation for this hotel."

Connor laughed out loud. "Yes, okay, you've got me there. But everything that happens from now on is unplanned. Okay?"

The bellman took their bags and they checked in. As soon as Shondra stepped into the gorgeous Mediterranean-style suite, she had a revelation. "Oh, no."

Connor turned. "What's wrong?"

"I just realized that none of my clothes are right for this trip. All I have are business suits." While everyone frolicked in their elegant beachwear, she'd be the only fool at the pool in a silk shirt and long pants.

Connor laughed, pulling out a credit card. "Don't worry. They have a fabulous gift shop downstairs. And if you don't like what they have there, Monte Carlo has legendary shopping."

Shondra waved him away. "I don't need your credit card. I have my own. I just wish I'd been able to plan better. I could have brought everything I need."

Connor put his credit card away, shaking his head. "You still haven't gotten the hang of living spontaneously. It's not about what could have been if you'd planned. It's about what's going to be because the mood strikes you."

Shondra inhaled and exhaled. This was going to take some getting used to. She couldn't help feeling it was wasteful to buy new clothes when she had all she needed at home. It wasn't about money, it was about practicality. Her father had demanded that the Braddock children wouldn't behave like over-privileged brats. They'd all worked and had responsibilities from early ages.

"Look," Connor said, seeing that she didn't know what to do with herself. "Why don't we run downstairs and find some things you like? Just enough to get you started, then we'll really shop tomorrow. When we get back, we can hit the casino."

"Fine. It can't hurt to check out what they have," Shondra said, throwing up her hands in surrender. "But I can go by myself. I know men don't really like to watch women shop."

Connor raised his brows suggestively. "Don't be so sure."

"No, you stay here and unpack. I'll be back before you can miss me."

Connor waited until Shondra had left the room before pulling out his cell phone. It had been vibrating out of control ever since their plane landed. The call log showed almost a dozen messages from his ex-girlfriend, Valerie.

They'd known each other since they were teenagers, but for the last ten years they'd had an on-again, off-again relationship. Some called it friendship with benefits. In any case, nothing that warranted an immediate response. On the other hand, Connor couldn't imagine Valerie working so hard to reach him for a booty call.

As he contemplated the wisdom of returning Valerie's calls before his weekend getaway was over, the phone vibrated again. This time it was his father. He couldn't ignore this call.

"Yeah, Dad?"

"You took the company jet. The pilot says you're in Monte Carlo."

"Yes. We've had a good week. I decided to take a long weekend," Connor said stiffly. He knew what was coming.

"I assume you're not alone."

He rolled his eyes. "No, I'm with a friend. And before you ask, I still have the right to privacy in my *personal* life."

It was hard to keep the resentment out of his voice. His father breathed down his neck at the office. Nothing was ever good enough. But unless he wanted to chuck everything he'd worked for out the window, he had to put up with it. He wasn't going to stand for his father's high-handedness about his dates.

"Yes, well, it's not my fault your personal life has landed on my doorstep."

Connor started. "What do you mean?"

"Valerie came by the office this afternoon looking for you."

"So?" He said the word casually but he was starting to get a sinking feeling.

"She was in a frantic state—saying she had to reach you urgently. You haven't gotten her in trouble have you?"

He scoffed. "You'd love that, wouldn't you? You and Woody pray for the day Valerie and I get married. And that would be just the excuse you needed to make it happen."

Carl Stewart and Woodrow Cardone had both made their money in the oil industry, one in drilling, the other in refinery. They were lifelong friends and had been pushing their children together for as long as Connor could remember, hoping to make their kinship official.

"In any case, you still haven't answered my question. Do you know why she's trying to reach you?"

"I don't know, but I'm sure it's not what you're thinking. Valerie and I are just friends."

"I know that's what you say, but the longer you play the field the more you're going to realize that women like Valerie don't come along often."

Connor disagreed. He knew a lot of women like Valerie. Rich, bored and always looking for that next big thrill. The only reason he went back to her so often was that she viewed relationships like a man—with cold pragmatism.

It was actually the reason they'd given up trying to make a real relationship out of what they had. It had been too exhausting trying to get her to settle down.

Now they didn't need candles or drawn-out

foreplay. When it was convenient, they hooked up. Period. And even that hadn't been a recent occurrence.

But he couldn't explain any of that to his father. "I'll call her and find out what she wants, Dad. But don't get your hopes up for any shotgun weddings. Valerie treats a sale at Bloomingdale's like an emergency."

"I'll give you this weekend. But when you get back, I want your mind focused on work. You promised to make Stewart Industries your priority. I don't expect to hear of any more long weekends for a while. A man doesn't build a business on vacation."

Connor hung up, barely resisting the urge to throw the phone off the balcony.

Was becoming CEO really worth all this? He loved the family business and even if he could do anything else in the world, Connor couldn't imagine working outside the oil industry.

He had ideas that flowed with the changing times. If he could just get his father to listen, the latest engineering technology showed that there were ways to process oil that were safer and more environmentally sound.

But his father and his cronies were locked in

tradition and doing things the old way. He couldn't start really funding these new methods until his father turned the company over to him completely.

And unfortunately, that meant tighter and tighter hoops to jump through until his father couldn't deny him any longer. Connor just hoped he could bring the old man around before he had to make any life-altering sacrifices.

Punching in Valerie's number on speed dial, he wasn't surprised when she answered on the first ring.

"Where have you been? I've left you a hundred messages."

"I know. What could possibly be urgent enough for you to visit my father—"

"I'm pregnant."

Chapter 6

Connor felt a chill wash over him despite the beads of sweat that prickled on his upper lip. "Excuse me?"

Valerie released a cold laugh. "You heard me. I'm pregnant."

"You're not trying to imply that— We haven't been together in over—"

"Of course it's not your baby, Connor."

The jolt of relief he felt was so strong his knees almost buckled. "Then why the hell were you so anxious to reach me? I'm sure it's wonderful news, but is it really an emergency?"

"You have no idea what I've been through. Alejandro has disappeared, and I'm pretty sure Daddy had something to do with it."

Connor's jaw dropped. "You think your father killed your boyfriend?"

Valerie snorted. "No. Of course not. He bought him off. He hired a private investigator and found out that Alejandro works at the Blue Planet."

"Isn't that a strip joint?"

"It's a high-end burlesque theater. Alejandro has a real gift for dance. He used to work in one of the Cirque du Soleil shows in Vegas."

Connor didn't waste his time arguing. He just needed this conversation over. "Anyway, you think Woody paid Alejandro to disappear."

"It wouldn't be the first time, and it's the only logical explanation. I haven't heard from Alejandro in three days, he's quit his job and his apartment has been cleaned out."

Connor thought about how much the family image meant to Woody. He'd gone to great lengths to end Valerie's friendship with Paris Hilton because he didn't like the fact that cameras followed her around. "Are you *sure* Woody didn't have him killed?" He laughed.

"This is no time for jokes, Connor."

"Okay, I'm sorry," he said, getting serious. "Why did you call me? Do you want me to help track down Alejandro so you can tell him about the baby?"

"No. Goodbye and good riddance. I can't raise a child with a man who can't stand up to my father."

Connor couldn't argue with that. "So what do you want from me?"

"I want you to marry me of course."

Shondra woke feeling more relaxed and rested than she had since her father's death. As she sat up against the down-filled pillows, she was seized by a wave of guilt. Somehow feeling this happy seemed wrong.

They'd stayed up late into the night at the casino, despite the fact that Shondra was convinced Connor was a bit preoccupied with work. She wasn't much of a gambler, but Connor had taken it upon himself to take her around and give her a little taste of each game. And even though they lost a fair amount of money, Shondra had had the time of her life.

But in the back of her mind, she'd known she didn't have any business gallivanting around Monte Carlo without a care in the world.

At least when she was working or conducting her investigation, she was doing something productive. Right now she was being completely selfish. Before she could let herself fall into a downward spiral, Shondra reminded herself of Connor's words from the night before.

This weekend is a fantasy and we're going to lose ourselves in it. Our troubles don't exist. While we're here, we're the only two people in the world.

Connor had probably anticipated the fact that she would feel a bit guilty for enjoying herself when she was still in mourning. He had been giving her permission to let those negative feelings go.

As if on cue, Connor emerged from the bathroom wearing nothing but a towel around his waist. "I filled up the whirlpool bath. Wanna take a soak with me?"

Taking a deep breath, Shondra filled her eyes with his smooth golden muscles. *We're the only two people in the world,* she told herself as she climbed out of bed and walked into Connor's arms.

By the time they had dressed, it was nearly time for lunch. Nevertheless, they ate their breakfast on the terrace overlooking the Mediterranean Sea. When they'd eaten their fill of eggs, waffles and fresh fruit, Connor instructed Shondra to grab a bathing suit and said he'd take care of the rest.

The white string bikini Shondra had found in the gift shop was much more revealing than the one she normally wore. But Europeans had no use for modesty, so Shondra decided to go for it.

Shondra hadn't known what to expect, maybe a private cabana by the pool or massages on the beach, but when Connor led her down to the docks, she found herself boarding a beautiful yacht.

He introduced her to the captain, and then led her to the upper deck where Connor got behind the bar and started mixing a cocktail for her.

The sun was high and beating down hot, so Shondra loosened a few buttons on her white sleeveless polo. "I can't believe you rented a yacht for us," she said as he handed her a pink drink in a martini glass.

"I didn't rent it. I own it."

Shondra rolled her eyes. "You keep a yacht in Monte Carlo? Of course. What was I thinking?"

Connor laughed. "Get in your bathing suit, then we can take our drinks to the sun deck and lie out."

Shondra turned and looked at him as if he were crazy.

"What?" he asked, noticing her look.

"I don't *lie* out."

His expression was blank for a second then realization passed over his face. A pink tinge rose on his cheeks. "Oh, sorry. You probably aren't trying to tan, are you?" he said. laughing.

She shook her head. "It's okay though, I brought my SPF 40. Maybe if you have an umbrella or something, I could sit in the shade while *you* tan."

Connor did find an umbrella and they settled on the sundeck. Shondra had never really understood the pleasures of sunbathing, but watching Connor was giving her a new appreciation for it.

She helped him apply a liberal coating of sunscreen and then watched him discard his red trunks and stretch out on the deck chair. His muscled buttocks sparkled in the sun and Shondra watched his every flex and shift the way she watched the evening news.

After an hour of sailing, the boat docked in the middle of the ocean and the captain appeared to tell Connor that they could go for a swim if they wished.

Shondra's heartbeat sped up. She hadn't come prepared to get her hair wet. Black men barely understood a black woman's struggle with her hair, so she really didn't want to get into that with Connor.

She also didn't want to spoil his fun. Connor might think she was a drag—not carefree, without hang-ups about tanning or hairstyles like other women.

He must have read the trepidation in her face because he said, "Come here."

Shondra silently followed him into the yacht, to the master bedroom. At first she thought he wanted to make love, but he ducked into a marble-lined bathroom. Pulling open a drawer, he showed her curling irons, combs, brushes, clips and a hair dryer.

"Did you buy all this for me?"

Connor laughed. "My mother used to sail on this yacht, and she used to require the full gambit of beauty supplies. I remembered that, so I wanted to make sure I afforded you that same benefit."

Shondra's heart filled. In the short time she'd known him, Connor had never failed to anticipate her needs. It was a bit unnerving, but it touched her completely.

Shondra jumped into his arms. Connor welcomed her kisses, eventually falling back on the king-size bed behind them. It took them quite a while to remember their swim.

But when they finally got around to it, the cool water revitalized them. Floating in the middle of the ocean with no other boats around, Shondra had begun to believe they *were* the only two people in the world—the only two people that mattered, anyway.

Back on the yacht, they let the sun dry their bodies and Shondra didn't even mind her skin's new sun-enriched tint. Afterward, they showered and changed. It was early evening when they arrived back at the hotel.

The sun had drained her energy, leaving her lethargic. "Connor, can we order room service? I don't think I'm up for all the fanfare of fine dining tonight." She flopped backward onto the bed, determined not to move.

"I'm sorry, hon. I have something special in mind for tonight."

Shondra lifted her head. She was starving. They'd had such a late breakfast, they'd decided to skip lunch altogether. "Do I have to dress up?"

To her relief Connor shook his head. "You can wear exactly what you have on now."

She looked down at the faded jeans and T-shirt she'd changed into after their swim. If this outfit was appropriate, then they really *weren't* going anywhere fancy. Maybe he wanted to show her he could do hamburgers and fries like the best of them. "Okay, I'm in. Where are we going for dinner?"

"When you get up, I'll show you."

With a sigh, Shondra peeled herself off the bed and followed Connor out of the room, down the elevator and straight for the main dining room. "But I thought you said—"

"Shh. Don't worry."

Shondra cringed when they walked past the maitre d' before crossing the restaurant. She followed, keeping her head down, not wanting to call attention to her poor attire.

At the back of the restaurant, Connor pushed through the kitchen doors.

"What's going on?"

Connor ignored her as he was met by what had to be the head chef. They exchanged a few words in French before Connor introduced her. Then the chef led them over to an empty workspace in the bustling kitchen.

"I'm going to prove to you that I can cook.

And, at the same time, I'm going to give you a little cooking lesson."

Shondra was dumbstruck. "Right now? In *this* kitchen?"

Connor laughed. "There's no time like the present."

He handed her a tomato. "You do know how to chop vegetables, don't you?"

"I understand the concept. I can't promise not to cut myself," she said, eyeing the large, extremely sharp knife he handed her.

"Let me get you started. You have to tuck your fingers in like this. That way you won't cut yourself." He quickly diced the tomato then handed her another one to try.

Shondra followed his orders as he handed her vegetables to chop while he sautéed shrimp and mushrooms in a pan. She boiled some fresh pasta and finally helped him to toss it with the vegetables and fresh herbs she'd prepared.

Connor artfully arranged the food on two plates. "There you have it," he said, handing her a plate. "Your first cooking lesson and a hot meal."

"It smells fantastic," Shondra said, unable to hide her grin. Of all the romantic gestures Connor had shown her during the short time they'd been together, this was the most impressive. He could have had a fancy meal catered for the two of them from anywhere in town, but he'd made arrangements to make them a delicious meal with his own two hands.

Shondra couldn't help finding it endearing that he'd grown up with all the privileges in the world, but he wasn't ever too good to get his hands dirty. She'd met men with much less money that weren't so down-to-earth.

They carried their plates back to their hotel suite and made mixed drinks from the minibar. Eating on the surface of the expansive bedspread was very much like having a picnic.

From their open hotel curtains they could see the sparkling city lights of Monte Carlo stretching out to the black of the sea. Shondra couldn't think of a more romantic date.

After dinner, Connor disappeared to take another shower and Shondra picked up her cell phone to check for messages. There were four texts, two from each of her brothers. They wanted to know where she was and the status of her investigation.

Guilt stabbed Shondra right through the heart. It felt wrong to be investigating the man she was sleeping with. Every instinct she had told her Connor was trustworthy. If someone at Stewart Industries did have something to do with her father's death, then it had to be someone other than Connor.

Shondra's gaze drifted to the bathroom door. Maybe she should confide in him? With Connor's help, she'd have direct access to the information she needed. Her brothers wouldn't appreciate her involving an outsider, but sometimes it was impossible to work alone.

With a heavy sigh, Shondra weighed her options. If she could trust Connor with her secrets, their relationship could be more honest. Shondra wouldn't have to feel like she was sneaking around behind his back. They would have a shot at a relationship that could last. And Shondra was starting to believe that was something she really wanted.

But what if the person connected to her father's death was someone close to Connor? It could even be his father, Carl Stewart. What if involving Connor in her investigation made him vulnerable in some way?

Shondra didn't like that scenario. If Carl Stewart was involved in shady dealings that somehow led to her father's death, that would put *her* in immediate danger. He would have connected her family name with Harmon Braddock from the start. No, it had to be someone much further down on the corporate ladder, if there was a connection at all.

She also had to consider the possibility that the anonymous call was a prank.

Shondra's head started to pound with all the stresses weighing on her mind. She didn't know what was the right thing to do. Maybe Connor could help her sort it out. It wouldn't hurt to feel him out on the topic.

But all of that would have to wait until morning. She was too tired even to wait for Connor to get out of the shower.

In the light of day, she'd be able to make a clearheaded decision.

Shondra awoke Sunday morning to find Connor missing from their bed. Assuming he was in the bathroom, she pulled on one of the fluffy white hotel robes and went to look over the room-service menu. As she retrieved it from the desk, she saw that the bathroom door was wide-open.

A cursory inspection showed that Connor was

nowhere to be found. Before she could panic, she saw that the balcony door was cracked open.

Shondra went to pull it all the way open and paused.

Connor was outside talking on his cell phone and his voice was urgent.

"I'm not going to let you blackmail me. There's no way I can do what you're asking. Besides, my father's not going to take your word over mine."

Shondra backed away from the door, stunned. Blackmail? It seemed Connor had secrets of his own.

Shrugging off her robe, she climbed back into bed. She didn't know what he was mixed up in, but she didn't want him to know she'd overheard any part of his conversation.

Shondra chided herself for being so blindly trusting. Clearly there were a lot of things she didn't know about Connor. If he'd put himself in a position to be blackmailed, she couldn't afford to trust him with her secrets. She was going to have to tread very carefully from now on.

Less than a minute later, Connor returned. "Good morning, sweetheart," he said, leaning down to brush his lips against hers lightly. "Did you just wake up?"

Shondra saw Connor with new eyes. Now she could see the strain in the tightly corded muscles of his neck. She remembered those moments over the last two days when he'd zoned out, a pained expression on his face. Now she could see that Connor's constant reminders to block out the outside world were not for her. He'd been trying to convince himself.

"Good morning. I just opened my eyes." She watched his face. "Where were you?"

"I was out on the balcony getting some fresh air and checking out the weather. Looks like it's going to be a beautiful day."

"Really? I thought I heard voices."

"You caught me…"

Shondra caught her breath. He was going to tell her the truth.

"I was talking to myself. I hope that's not what woke you."

"No," she said, feeling her heart sink into her chest. Whatever was going on with him, he didn't trust her with it.

She'd been about to lay all her secrets on the table before him. That would have been a huge mistake. Shondra had no idea what this relationship meant to him. They hadn't made each other any promises. For all she knew, Connor did this kind of thing all the time. Had she been naive to think she was special?

"This is our last day in Monte Carlo. We can do anything you want. Gambling, sailing, shopping, you name it."

Shondra chewed her lip. Connor was in some kind of trouble. She hoped it wasn't the kind of trouble that could get him hurt. But she believed Connor could take care of himself.

And she had to take care of *her*self. How could she stay another day and pretend things hadn't changed? She couldn't.

She shouldn't have agreed to come in the first place. But she'd allowed herself to get caught up in the fantasy. Now she saw things far too clearly to play along anymore.

"Actually, I think I'd like to fly back to Houston."

Connor's face registered surprise. "What? Why? You're not expected back to the office until Tuesday."

"It's been a lovely weekend, but I have a lot of things I've neglected at home. And my family has these big dinners at least once a month. It's a tradition my father started and we're trying to keep it going. They'll be expecting me back for that."

After a moment Connor nodded. "If that's what you want. I'll make the arrangements. By the time you're dressed and packed, the plane should be ready to go."

Two hours later they were sitting opposite each other on the company jet. An uncomfortable silence was stretching out between them. It was a far cry from the atmosphere of their previous flight.

Shondra stared into the screen of her PDA, trying to avoid Connor's gaze. Ever since she'd started packing that morning, there had been a growing pain in her stomach. She couldn't believe she was making herself physically sick over a man.

What a difference a day made. When he'd joined her in bed the night before, she'd tucked into his arms and had slept peacefully. Today, she'd awakened to realize she didn't really know the man across from her.

"Shondra," Connor whispered her name.

She held her breath for a second before looking up.

He nodded to her PDA. "Can you put that down for a minute? I want to talk to you. You've barely said a word since we boarded the plane."

She put her PDA on the table between them. "I'm sorry. I didn't mean to be antisocial. It's just that whirlwind weekends away have consequences. I still have responsibilities."

Shondra heard the coldness in her words and embraced it. Looking into Connor's perfect face, she was tempted to continue playing the fool. It would be so much easier to ignore her fears and spend the next few hours naked in his arms.

"I can tell something's wrong. What is it? Is it your father?"

Her shoulders hunched. She'd been so quick to dismiss his involvement in her father's death. "What do you know about my father?"

Connor stared at her, puzzled. He shrugged. "I know what you told me. What's going on?"

Her shoulders slumped. Until she'd gotten involved with Connor, Shondra had kept her relationships simple and stress free. It was true she didn't get to experience the thrilling roller coaster of emotions Connor brought about. But when the relationships were over, she experienced very little pain.

"I just don't think I can do this anymore."

"You don't think you can do what?"

"Us." Shondra held her stomach as the ache intensified. "I don't think this relationship has a future. I think we both know that, and it's best for the both of us if we go ahead and admit that now."

Chapter 7

Connor heard Shondra's words, but they took a moment to sink in. She was dumping him?

He scolded himself for his surprise. Shondra had been distant all morning. Then, out of the blue, she'd announced she wanted to go home. It was as if she'd woken up a different woman.

Fear pierced his heart. Could she have overheard him on the phone this morning? Biting his lip, he forced himself to push that thought aside. He couldn't explain things, even if she had.

Valerie wanted him to marry her and had made it clear that she wouldn't be taking no for an answer. Even though he'd tried his best to talk sense to her, she'd kept insisting that their marriage would be a win-win situation.

It hadn't taken long for Connor to realize it was a problem he had to take care of in person. Hopefully, by the time he got back to Houston, she'd have gotten hold of her senses.

But he had to manage one problem at a time.

"So, you're breaking up with me? Just like that? Thanks for the great weekend in Monte Carlo, but it's over?"

Shondra winced. "No, not just like that. This isn't where I wanted to end up. I really like you. And this weekend was like a fairy tale."

She looked down at her hands. "If we could stay in a fairy tale for the rest of our lives, I'd be willing. But in the real world, our relationship is complicated. The fact that I work for you, my father's recent death—these are all things that I just can't juggle right now."

Connor shook his head. She hadn't even mentioned the fact that they were from different races. It hadn't become a problem because they'd been keeping their relationship a secret. As much as he hated to admit it, Connor knew there were people in his father's circle who would have a problem with him dating a black woman. But he wasn't the kind of guy who ran away from trouble.

He opened his mouth to tell her just that when Valerie's words echoed in his head. *I'm pregnant and I want you to marry me*.

Staring out the airplane window, he cursed under his breath. Shondra was just scared. And normally he wouldn't let something like that stand in his way. He would pretend to give in, and then do whatever it took to win her back. But he wasn't quite free to do that now.

The last thing he needed right now was to make Shondra promises he couldn't keep. And if she found out about Valerie before he had a chance to set her straight, he'd never get another chance with Shondra.

He slumped back into his seat, defeated. "I know you're right" was all he could say.

Shondra blinked at him. Clearly she'd been expecting him to put up more of a fight. And it was killing him that he couldn't.

"My father would definitely prefer I focus on the future of Stewart Industries instead of my love life," he offered in explanation. Connor ran a hand through his hair. "This isn't what I want.

But I can respect the fact that you're not ready to take all of this on."

Shondra nodded. "It was only a matter of time before the entire office found out about us."

Connor shrugged. It was strange not being in the driver's seat anymore. "So, where do we go from here? Do we pretend that we're still going to be friends?"

"I don't think that's a good idea. We still have to work together...."

"Right. A working relationship, then." He leaned his head against the window, rubbing his temple.

Everything good in his life was starting to unravel. And he'd be damned if he let Valerie get away with pulling the string.

Shondra walked through her front door to the frantic sound of dogs yipping and barking. Slamming the door shut, she dropped her luggage in the foyer. "Lisa!"

Seconds later Lisa dashed down the stairs, a horrified look on her face. "Oh my God. Shondra, you weren't supposed to be back until tomorrow."

She rolled her eyes. "Let me guess. We have a few houseguests."

"Just three very small, very well-behaved Chihuahuas," Lisa said, her eyes pleading.

"Three?"

"Yes, their mom paid me a hundred dollars extra to take them home with me. They don't like to be separated. And the kennel doesn't allow more than one dog to a cage. So…bringing them here was the only humane thing for me to do."

Shondra looked into Lisa's ashen face and sighed.

"I'll split the hundred with you," Lisa said hopefully.

Shondra waved her off. Suddenly she didn't care anymore. What difference did it make?

"No, it's okay. Just don't let them in my bedroom. And if I see any dog poo—"

Lisa threw her arms around her. "Say no more. You have my word of honor. It will be like they're not even here."

Shondra pried herself free. "I seriously doubt that."

Shondra followed Lisa to her bedroom where the three little dogs had made themselves at home. One was curled like a little princess on the bedspread. Another was on the floor quietly chewing on Lisa's slipper and the third had run up to Shondra and was jumping up and down for her attention.

"That's Sophie. She wants you to pick her up," Lisa said.

Giving in, despite her better judgment, Shondra leaned down and scooped the dog into her arms. "What's with the little T-shirts? It's nearly eighty degrees outside. They can't be cold."

"Their mom likes for them to be fashion forward."

Shondra held little Sophie away from her face as the dog started to lick her. This situation was already out of control. She hated owners who thought they could be parents to another species. She hated animals dressed in cutesy clothing. And she hated face-licking.

And yet, after the way she'd come home feeling, a little unconditional love from a creature that didn't even know her was exactly what Shondra needed.

"You must have had one heck of a business trip. You're more mellow that usual."

Shondra smiled up at her friend. "Mellow isn't the word I would use." Melancholy? Morose? *Mental*—that was more like it.

Lisa leaned closer, studying Shondra carefully. "Something's going on? Did you meet some hot Latin lover in Venezuela or is that delicious boss of yours the reason for your relaxed glow?"

Shondra blinked in surprise. Apparently there was a fine line between beaming serenity and feeling emotionally comatose.

"Turns out the business trip was canceled. But rather than call me and tell me that, Connor arranged a spontaneous trip to Monte Carlo. We spent the weekend in a luxury hotel and soaking up sun on his yacht."

Lisa pouted. "I definitely got out of law too soon. The firm I worked for didn't have dream bosses like yours." She flopped down on her bed and focused her laser-sharp gaze on Shondra. "That sounds like it came straight out of *Love's Paradise.* Tell me everything."

Lisa had every spare surface of her bedroom stacked and piled with romance novels. She was holding out for her own real-life romantic hero and did nightly research between those pages. Maybe Shondra should start borrowing from Lisa's collection because that was the only romance she'd be getting from now on.

Shondra stared down into the loving brown

eyes of the dog she was holding. No wonder dogs were man's best friends. That was loyalty. "I hate to tell you this, Lisa, but these romantic getaways aren't all they're cracked up to be."

Lisa sat up. "Why not? What happened?"

"What happens is that you eventually have to come back to the real world."

"Who says?" Lisa joked, then changed gears when she saw Shondra's face. "Didn't you have a good time?"

"The weekend was amazing. But Connor and I have the kind of relationship that doesn't hold up outside of the fantasy."

"That's nonsense. Relationships are work. You haven't given it enough time to know what you two could have together."

"This just isn't the right time for me, Lisa." She couldn't tell her friend what she was really doing at Stewart Industries. It wasn't that she didn't trust her, but this was a family matter.

"My father just died. I can't trust any of the emotions I'm having right now. I have a new job with a lot of responsibility. Plus, if I focus my energies anywhere it should be on my family, not a man I barely know."

Lisa stared at Shondra quietly.

Her silent, stony face made Shondra uncomfortable. "What?"

"I want to point something out to you, but I want you to promise we'll still be friends afterward."

Shondra felt a stab of apprehension. "Of course."

"Okay. Good."

"What do you want to tell me?"

"Do you know why you normally date guys that aren't in your league?"

Shondra bristled. "That's a little harsh. I don't buy into the class system—"

"It's not because you're being rebellious, like you think."

"What do you mean? I never said—"

"It's because you're playing it safe. You date men you can control. Men that don't challenge you. Connor is the first man you've dated who's your equal, and I'm not talking about money. All your life you've avoided strong, powerful men. Men like the ones in your family."

Shondra blinked. That wasn't true. It couldn't be. She liked men who worked with their bodies. Men who weren't afraid to get their hands dirty. That was her taste.

"Lisa, thanks for the bedspread psychoanalysis. But that's just not true."

"Really? Because your relationship with Connor is the first one you've ever had to put any effort into. It sounds to me like you're scared and you're running away."

Shondra stubbornly shook her head. "It's so much more complicated than that." The dog in her arms yipped, probably from being held too tight, and she had to put her down.

"Okay," Lisa said. "I'll let you get away with it for now. Just remember, if you need to lean on anyone, you always have me."

Shondra hugged her friend. She didn't need a man. She already had everything she needed.

Shondra was grateful that she wasn't expected at work Monday morning, because she didn't feel like facing the possibility of seeing Connor. Now she knew exactly why office romances were discouraged.

Even though it had been her idea to break things off, she still woke up feeling completely out of sorts. It was going to take her all day just to save up enough energy to meet her family for dinner that evening.

Shondra slogged around the house with none of her normal energy. She went to Lisa's room and played with the dogs. She knew Lisa was eyeing her as though she'd grown a second head, but Shondra didn't care.

Maybe she'd get a dog of her own. Just then Sophie smiled up at her and peed on her sneaker. Jumping back with a shriek, she pulled off the offending shoe. "Lisa—"

"I know. I owe you a new pair of sneakers."

"You've got that right."

By the time seven o'clock rolled around, Shondra was ready to jump out of her skin. Lazing around the house all day just wasn't for her. She'd alternated between wishing she'd stayed in Monte Carlo the extra day and wishing she'd gone into the office.

Anxious to have somewhere to go, she climbed into her navy-blue Mercedes and headed to the Braddock estate. She could make the trip in her sleep, so it took a while to notice that a dark car was tailgating.

Checking her speedometer, Shondra noted that she was going about ten miles over the limit. Not in the mood to play traffic games, she slowed down and changed lanes.

The car sped past and Shondra exited the highway. Less than ten minutes later she pulled into her parents' long curving drive.

There were extra cars parked in front of the house and Shondra braced herself. It wasn't just going to be family. Great. She was barely in the mood to deal with her brothers, let alone friends of her father's.

Shondra knew it was for the best. Her mother needed the constant flow of guests that had been in and out of the mansion since Harmon Braddock's death. The most frequent visitors were her father's closest friends, Senator Ray Cayman and Judge Bruce Hanlon.

Even after so many weeks, as Shondra walked into the foyer of her family home, a fresh wave of pain began to radiate in her chest. All the childhood images of jumping into her father's arms when he came through the door assailed her like old ghosts.

She couldn't imagine how her mother managed to continue living here, to continue sleeping in their bed without her husband. It took all of Shondra's energy not to get lost in the emptiness her father had left behind in the cavernous mansion.

She started down the hall, avoiding the urge

to look into her father's den where she would be haunted anew. Their housekeeper, Sarona, as much a fixture in the Braddock home as the stove, bustled from the kitchen to the parlor carrying a tray of hors d'oeuvres.

Shondra had only taken two more steps before her mother came out of the parlor to greet her.

Evelyn Braddock, former model turned philanthropic activist, had an ageless beauty that had led many to think she and Shondra were sisters. But since her husband's death, her sixty-two years had finally begun to show around her eyes.

"Shondra, honey. You look tired. Are you getting enough sleep?"

"I had the day off today, Mom. I got nothing but sleep."

Shondra followed her mother into the parlor where Malcolm was standing behind the bar mixing drinks. It was hard not to notice that he wasn't wearing his typical uniform of khakis and a button-down shirt. Instead he wore a stylish crew-neck sweater with jeans. Shondra knew the woman responsible for this transformation was Malcolm's girlfriend, Gloria Kingsley.

"Shawnie," Malcolm called as she neared him.

She knew it was a bit cowardly, and that she

was only postponing the inevitable, but Shondra decided to work the room before she faced her brother.

"Hi, Malcolm," Shondra said, waving as she passed. "I'll be right back."

The first person she spotted was Judge Bruce Hanlon. He had a warm, friendly face, blue eyes and silver hair. He was choosing one of Sarona's signature crab puffs from the serving tray as Shondra approached.

"Shondra," he said, leaning down to kiss her on the cheek. "It's so good to see you, dear. When Evelyn included me in this little gathering, she told me you might not be joining us."

She squeezed his arm affectionately. "I was supposed to be out of town, but luckily I was able to return earlier than expected."

"Well, it wouldn't have been the same without you, sweetheart," Judge Hanlon stated with his typical grandfatherly charm.

Shondra spent a few minutes answering Judge Hanlon's questions about her new job. No matter how busy he was, throughout the years he'd always taken the time to show an interest in her projects, and as a result she'd come to think of him as part of the family.

As they were talking, Senator Ray Cayman came over to join them. Tall, with freckled mahogany skin and salt-and-pepper hair, the senator had always seemed to Shondra as a bit of an imposing figure. She'd always felt he lacked Judge Hanlon's charm.

Greeting him politely, Shondra quickly excused herself to find Gloria. As she reached her side, Gloria turned to give her a friendly hug. She'd known her father's executive assistant for years, but ironically, it wasn't until after his death that Gloria had completely become involved in Braddock family gatherings.

In her trendy tan cocktail dress, Gloria glimmered from the golden highlights frosting her light brown cap of hair to her flashing golden eyes.

Never one to mince words, Gloria took Shondra's arm and whispered in her ear, "I can tell you're avoiding him, but you're going to have to talk to him eventually. You may as well get it over with."

Shondra laughed. "I don't know what you're talking about. I was just greeting our guests. There's no reason for me to avoid my older brother."

"I'm glad to hear that because your time is up. Here he comes now."

Gloria kissed Malcolm on the cheek then slipped away, leaving Shondra on her own.

Malcolm hugged his sister and handed her a rum and Coke. "I haven't heard from you all weekend. Any news?"

Shondra took a long sip from her glass. "Not since I talked to you last. When I find something concrete, I'll tell you. You have to realize it's going to take some time."

"The more time it takes, the colder the trail gets, Shawnie. I'm starting to think it might be better if we—"

Before he could finish, Tyson showed up. As it had been the last time they'd all gotten together, Tyson had arrived without his wife, Felicia. In fact, it had been quite some time since she'd made an appearance. Shondra couldn't help wondering if there was a problem in their marriage.

Tyson walked over, loosening his tie and shrugging out of his suit coat. He hugged them each hello. "Sorry I'm late. I was tied up at the office. I think I can guess what the two of you are talking about."

Malcolm quickly brought him up to speed, and now that Tyson had joined the conversation, Shondra knew she was outnumbered.

"Maybe you shouldn't have taken on this responsibility, Shawnie," Tyson said, trading a heavy look with Malcolm. "Things are more complicated now. Have you told her, Malcolm?"

Shondra turned expectant eyes to her oldest brother. With a heavy sigh he said, "When Gloria and I went to clean up Dad's office we found the place ransacked."

Shondra's jaw dropped. "Oh, no! Was anything missing?"

Tyson shook his head as Malcolm answered. "We couldn't find anything missing, but someone was clearly looking for something specific. We just don't know what. I think it's time we turned this over to the professionals. Drey St. John has offered to look into this for us. Maybe we should take him up on his offer?"

Shondra rolled her eyes. Drey St. John was a private investigator her father had been associated with. "I'm sorry to hear about Dad's office, but I don't think we should involve any more people in this situation than we have to. At least not yet."

"Drey's already involved…and this is what he does for a living."

She'd had enough. Shondra had sacrificed a lot and she wasn't ready to have it all amount to nothing. "Just give me some time. Stewart Industries is a big company with a lot of holdings. But I'm on the inside. Right now, that's an advantage we can't afford to squander. I'll find out if they have a connection with Dad's accident. But I've got to tread lightly here. When I get some information, you two will be the first to know. Until then, you've got to trust me."

Before her brothers could respond, Senator Cayman began tapping on his glass to get the room's attention. "Excuse me for interrupting your conversations, but Judge Hanlon and I have joined the Braddocks here this evening because I believe an important announcement is going to be made. Malcolm?"

Shondra turned to her brother in surprise. He smiled sheepishly and walked to the front of the room.

"Thanks, Senator Cayman, you've saved me the trouble of trying to find just the right moment to do this. It's official—I've decided to run for congress in a special election and take over my father's seat in the House."

Shondra had been certain that after Malcolm's big news, she'd be off the hook for the rest of the night. No such luck. Senator Cayman and Judge Hanlon had only stopped by for Malcolm's announcement. And without the protection of guests at the table, Shondra found herself subjected to the usual relationship interrogation.

"Are you seeing anyone right now?" her mother asked her halfway through dinner.

Shondra had never been able to lie to her parents, and as much as she wanted to, now wasn't any different.

"I was seeing someone recently, but it's over now." She felt all the eyes in the room narrow in on her.

"Who was it?" Tyson asked.

"Does it matter?" Malcolm chimed in. "She said it was over."

"Who was it?" Tyson repeated his question, ignoring their older brother.

Shondra rolled her eyes. She couldn't tell them it was Connor Stewart. "C.J.," she said finally. "When I met him, he was working on an oil rig."

Fortunately that bit of information was enough to satisfy them. They'd never make the leap from C.J. to Connor James Stewart. Instead they got caught up admonishing her, as usual, on her taste in men.

"You know what you need, Shondra?" Tyson offered.

"Do tell. I'm on pins and needles," she said blandly.

"You need to date a man who can keep you interested. I know you don't like pencil pushers, but there's more to life than gardeners and garbage collectors."

Shondra was gearing up to call her brother a snob when Malcolm intervened. "You should let me introduce you to Randall Whitman. He plays football for the Dallas Cowboys. I met him at a fund-raising event a few weeks ago. He's out on medical leave for a shoulder injury. I think you two would get along."

Picturing Connor, Shondra started to protest. But she paused before she could get the words out. Connor was history, and this was the second time in two days someone close to her had questioned her choice of men. Her track record was lousy.

Maybe it wouldn't hurt to try dating someone new. At the very least, it would keep her mind off Connor.

"Okay," Shondra said finally. "Why don't you give Randall Whitman my number?"

There were shocked expressions aimed at Shondra from around the table. But for the first time that evening, she was able to enjoy her meal.

Chapter 8

Shondra stepped out of her family home rubbing her temples. The evening couldn't have ended soon enough for her. It had taken far too long to get the spotlight focused on someone other than herself. As the youngest and the only girl, there was always an endless stream of advice and judgment to put up with.

As she climbed into her sedan and started the engine, Shondra's thoughts were still wrapped up in her swirling emotions. Had she really just agreed to let her brother set her up? With a football player, no less? She didn't have the first clue about football. It had been an impulsive decision that she was already questioning.

The only good thing about embracing her family's constant meddling was that it had completely disarmed them. No one had been able to say another word about her judgment for the rest of the evening.

Shondra backed down the long winding driveway into the darkened street.

It was comforting to know they cared about her enough to lose sleep over her well-being. On the other hand, it was tough to make mistakes knowing that each family member would have an opinion about it. Maybe it wouldn't hurt to follow their advice for a change. Lord knew she wasn't doing a great job on her own. Maybe she and the football player would actually hit it off.

Shondra absently navigated the back roads out of the neighborhood, barely aware that a car had pulled out behind her.

Despite her forced optimism, her mind couldn't help drifting back to Connor. She'd thrown caution to the wind and had allowed herself to have a passionate fling. While it had been a definite thrill to give in to pure sexual attraction, she couldn't deny that it came with a price. It wasn't supposed to hurt when a brief affair ended. They'd only been together for a weekend. Why did it feel like her heart was breaking?

Glancing into her rearview mirror, Shondra realized the car following her was driving a bit too close to her bumper. She couldn't make out the figure behind the wheel. *This again?*

Probably some half-drunk heiress on her way out to a party, Shondra thought uncharitably. They were just outside a gated community where some of the local celebrities lived. She decided to slow down and let the car pass.

To her surprise, the car behind her slowed, too. The poor fool was probably lost and trying to tailgate her way out of the winding maze of narrow streets. Frowning, Shondra made a last-minute right turn and pulled her car over to the curb.

The car raced around the bend and slammed full-force into the back of Shondra's car. It hit her so hard, the car rocked forward, slamming Shondra's forehead into the steering wheel.

When she finally got her wits about her and began to climb out of the car to confront her assailant, what she now recognized as a Lexus backed up and raced away from the scene.

Swearing viciously, Shondra strode around

the car to inspect the damage. Her entire back end was crushed into the trunk, but at least it was drivable. Jumping back into the car, Shondra dialed 911.

Trembling slightly as she waited for the police, Shondra no longer cared about her mixed-up love life. There was nothing like a case of hit-and-run to put life into perspective.

Connor paced around his living room, trying his best not to put his fist through a wall. He certainly wouldn't ever receive any nominations for sainthood, but he'd always been very careful not to get anyone pregnant. And he still hadn't.

And yet here he was with a pregnant ex-girlfriend standing in his home demanding marriage. Trying to negotiate rationally over the phone had been futile. Now Connor was hoping he could get through to her with a face-to-face discussion.

Valerie Cardone had always been selfish, but he never would have suspected that she'd trash his life just to save face. "Unbelievable," he shouted, stalking back and forth.

Valerie crossed her legs and shrugged. "My father will absolutely die if you don't make this right."

Feeling his temper spiking, Connor stared daggers at Valerie. "How many times do I have to tell you, this isn't my problem? You know it's not my baby. A paternity test will prove that. What will you do then?"

"You and I have been seen around together and have dated off and on since college. Everyone will believe it's yours. Especially if I tell them so. By the time the results of a paternity test come out, the damage will be done."

"And you think I'll just sit back and allow this?"

She leveled him with her calculating green gaze. "Save us both some trouble and accept your fate, Connor. Our fathers have always wanted us to get together. If we get married, we can both have what we want. Your father will finally make you CEO and my father will secure my inheritance. In the end, we both win."

Seeing her perched on his sofa like a mannequin, Connor was having trouble remembering what he'd ever seen in her. She looked as cold and brittle as glass with her professionally dyed blond streaks, nightclub makeup and her expensive jeans and T-shirt artfully designed to look tattered.

They'd had plenty of good times together. When they were young, they'd commiserated over the lofty expectations of their important fathers. They'd stayed out all night together and partied hard in rebellion. Connor had outgrown those wild times, but apparently Valerie hadn't.

"Valerie, it's not my fault that you made your father angry by dating a male stripper. It's not my fault you allowed that lowlife to get you pregnant. I know it would make your life easier if I marry you and claim your baby, but what about my life? Until yesterday, I was seeing someone."

"The black Barbie doll?" Valerie said dismissively. "I checked her out. Seems to me that you like to get a rise out of the old man, too."

"That's not true. My father doesn't even know about Shondra and me." Then his heartbeat sped up as he registered her words. "What do you mean, you checked her out?"

She gave him a cool smile. "I'm a resourceful girl."

"Listen, you stay as far away from her as possible. I've got enough problems with her without adding you to the mix."

"You know as well as I do that your father would absolutely hate the idea of you dating a black woman. Isn't that why you didn't tell him about her?"

"No, of course not. My relationships are none of *your* business or anyone else's."

"We can have an open marriage, Connor. I'll let you have your women on the side. All I want is your name for my baby. This way my father won't disinherit me for disgracing the family and your dad won't have to suffer the shame of *your* indiscretions."

"When were you raised, the fifties? Having a child out of wedlock is no longer the shocker it was in our parents' time. You can raise the child on your own. Look at Nicole Richie. A little scandal didn't hurt her."

"You forget that my father is *very* old-fashioned. If I don't clean this up before he finds out on his own, I'm out of the will. That's not acceptable."

"That's not my problem," Connor said, feeling like a broken record.

"I can make it your problem. Trust me on that."

Shondra wasn't prepared for how awkward her first day back at the office would be after an illicit retreat with the boss. She'd started her morning by dropping her car off at the dealership for repairs and picking up a rental car. Her nerves were still frayed from the accident.

Now, at the office, she was avoiding a different kind of collision. She turned every corner fearing the sight of that dirty-blond hair and those sparkling blue eyes. Her best defense was to sit in her office with her nose buried in codes and regulations. That strategy had worked fine until around noon when she was called down to Human Resources to fill out some health insurance forms.

As Shondra gathered up the paperwork that Mary, the HR department head, had just spent the better part of an hour going over with her, she couldn't help feeling a bit guilty. Was she really going to be with Stewart Industries long enough to take advantage of all these benefits?

Shondra was beginning to question whether it was nearing time to cut her losses and leave. There hadn't been any more anonymous calls declaring her father's death a murder, and she was running out of resources here at SI. So far every lead Shondra followed had turned up nothing. She hadn't met a single person who admitted knowing Harmon Braddock.

Shondra stood to leave Mary's office when someone knocked on the door. A tall, older woman with Asian features entered. "Mary, do you have an updated copy of the staff list? I've still got the old one."

"Sure, just give me a minute," Mary said, looking over to her. "Have you met Shondra Braddock? She's our new chief compliance officer. Shondra, this is Daiyu Longwei."

Shondra nodded to the other woman, who looked surprisingly startled to see her. "It's nice to meet you."

"And you, as well," Daiyu answered, looking markedly pale. Shondra would have bet money that she didn't at all agree it was nice to meet her.

Not wanting to waste any more time, Shondra took her paperwork and excused herself from the office. Still thinking about the odd woman in the HR office, Shondra didn't notice Connor stepping onto the elevator until it was too late.

She looked up, startled, feeling all the blood drain from her face as her heart started to race. But to her surprise, Connor didn't move into her personal space or tease her with his gibing wit. The lines around his mouth were pressed tightly together and his eyes were wary. He simply nodded to her then turned to watch the numbers on the elevator panel light up.

He stepped off two floors later, leaving Shondra very much alone.

Connor walked into his office and stopped dead. "Valerie. What are you doing here?"

She was sitting in his guest chair reading a magazine as if she had an appointment. "I wanted to stop by to take you to lunch."

"No thanks. Blackmail makes me lose my appetite," he said quietly as he shut his office door.

"Have you reconsidered my offer?"

"It hasn't even been twenty-four hours since we last spoke. I've barely had time to process all of this. Can't you find another sucker? I can't be the only fool your father will accept into the family."

"You have to stop thinking about this as a favor to me, and start seeing how it can benefit you."

"I think you're overestimating your value."

"Now that's where you're wrong," Valerie said, propping herself on the edge of his desk. "Just think how fast your daddy will hand over the reins of SI once we're married. He'll retire happily once he knows there's a strong family bond between SI and Cardone Oil."

"Great. Now I'm supposed to saddle myself with you so I can run a company that's rightfully mine to inherit anyway. Yeah, that makes perfect sense," Connor said, throwing his hands up.

Sinking into his leather chair, he laid his head in his hands. An image of Shondra in the elevator came to mind. Why did his life have to be so complicated right now? The last thing he wanted was for Shondra to find out about Valerie. The tension had been thick between them as it was.

Shondra was scared of what they could have together. And if he didn't have his hands full with Valerie, he might have had a shot at changing her mind.

"I'll give you until the end of the week to decide," Valerie said. "But keep in mind, the clock is ticking."

"The end of the week to decide my future— isn't that generous of you." He shook his head. "Maybe I'm not ready to give up on having a life of my own."

"Ah, the girl. Is she what has you holding out? You're still hoping you can convince Daddy to let you play with Black Barbie."

Something inside Connor snapped. "Stop calling her that. Valerie, I can't stand the sight of you right now. Just get out."

"That's okay," Valerie said, standing. "When

you get tired of playing with toys, you'll start to see this isn't such a bad deal."

Connor stared at Valerie, willing her to shut up and exit before he really lost control.

She paused with her hand on the doorknob. The self-satisfied smirk was finally gone, as she regarded him seriously for the first time.

"You know, love is just a myth. Just because someone says the words and goes through the motions doesn't make it real. So you're better off negotiating the best terms for yourself and making a merger that can get you what you really need. Tangible things. We can make this work, Connor. Think about it."

Shondra had just returned from HR when Sarah popped into her office. "Have you eaten yet? I was thinking about getting some sushi. Want to come?"

"Sure, I could use some fresh air," Shondra said, reaching for her purse.

"I knew I had to get out of the office as soon as Valerie showed up. She has this annoying habit of treating me like a waitress," Sarah said as they headed toward the elevator.

"Who's Valerie?"

"Connor's on-again, off-again girlfriend. I guess, as of today, they're on again. She hasn't been around in months."

Shondra felt her entire body run cold. Connor had a girlfriend? Suddenly she knew why he'd agreed to break things off so easily. He'd gotten what he'd wanted from her. Apparently he'd never intended to have anything more than a fling.

She was lucky to get out when she did.

As they walked down the street, Shondra tried to pay attention as Sarah chattered away about all the office gossip she knew. But it was difficult to hold up her end of the conversation. She felt as though the whole world could see the word *fool* stamped on her forehead.

Connor was a playboy. She'd known better than to get involved with a man like that, but like an idiot, she'd done it anyway. She'd wanted an adventure. Now that she'd had one, she wasn't sure she liked it.

Over lunch, Shondra eventually allowed herself to relax. She'd nearly forgotten the multitude of stressors that had been weighing on her mind that day.

So when she walked into her office and saw a sticky note on her monitor, her eyes almost passed over it without taking it in. But something about the angry red scrawl caught her attention.

The sticky note read, Back Off Bitch.

Chapter 9

Shondra stared at the note until the words began to make sense. It was a threat. With her heart pounding in both fear and anger, she stalked over to the bank of secretarial cubicals outside her office.

Walking into the first one she found, Shondra came up behind the woman who performed administrative duties for her department. "Diane!"

Shondra said the name so sharply, the woman jumped in her seat.

Clutching her heart, she looked up, her dark

eyes wide. "What's wrong? You nearly scared me to death."

Shondra forced her voice to sound calm. "Sorry, I didn't mean to startle you. I just wanted to know if you saw anyone enter my office while I was at lunch."

Diane gave her a sheepish look. "I'm sorry. I left for lunch right after you. What happened? Is something wrong?"

Shondra started to show her the sticky note and then thought better of it. If she told anyone she'd been threatened, she'd have to report the incident to HR, and there would be an investigation. Then she'd have to explain exactly what she thought someone wanted her to back off from.

"No, nothing's wrong. Someone left me a note and forgot to sign it. Now I don't know who to attribute the request to."

Diane's gaze went to the sticky note balled in Shondra's fist. "Do you want me to see if I recognize the handwriting?"

She took a step back. "That's okay, Diane. If it's important, I'm sure someone will get back to me."

Shondra went back to her office but she couldn't concentrate on anything but the note. Someone wanted her to back off. That meant there really was something for her to find. But she hadn't been able to dig up anything so far.

Who could have figured out that she was doing more than compliance at Stewart Industries? Maybe it was the Braddock name. While she was in HR she found out that the new staff list with her name on it hadn't been distributed until today.

It was possible that someone had seen her name on the list and figured out that she'd been looking for information about her father. It was someone here at Stewart Industries that had contacted her family the first time. It was that person she was looking for. Which meant it could be *that* person who didn't want to be found.

But why make the initial contact? One thing was certain, if Shondra was thinking of giving up, now she knew that she couldn't. Someone had ransacked her father's office looking for something. It was becoming quickly apparent that this mystery was gathering momentum.

Suddenly fear jolted her like an electric shock. What if her car accident last night hadn't been an accident? Her father had died in a car crash. Was that same fate intended for her?

With her heart hammering in her chest, Shondra picked up the phone to dial her brother Malcolm. But she paused mid-dial. If she told either of her brothers about this new chain of events, they'd insist she quit Stewart Industries right away.

Now that she finally had a reason to believe she was on the right track, she couldn't let anything derail her. She'd just have to ramp up her investigation. She needed to get the job done quickly so she *could* get out of there.

In the meantime, she'd just have to be much more careful.

Shondra took a new route home that night, trying to make sure she wasn't followed. When she made it home without incident, she went straight into her bedroom and collapsed.

Lisa popped her head through the door minutes later. "Hey, girl, someone doesn't waste any time getting back on the horse."

Shondra slowly raised her leaden head from the pillow. "What are you talking about?"

"Check the voice mail. You have a message from none other than Randall Whitman from the Dallas Cowboys. Honey, I sure wish I had your mojo."

Shondra let her head fall back down. "It's not

what you think. Malcolm gave him the number. It's a fix-up."

When Lisa remained silent, Shondra shifted so she could see her friend's face. "What?"

"Connor must have done a number on you."

She sat up. "What do you mean?"

"You agreed to a blind date. And not just any blind date—a date with someone one of your *brothers* picked out. I thought I'd never live to see the day."

Shondra waved her off. "Don't make such a big deal out of it. You're the one who said I pick men that don't challenge me. I'm getting out of my comfort zone."

"I'll say. I never would have pictured you with a football player. Some of those guys are just meatheads with money."

"Now who's being judgmental? Besides, Malcolm met Randall at a fund-raiser. You know Malcolm, he's the intellectual type—he wouldn't fix me up with a meathead."

Lisa snorted. "In any case, the date should be interesting."

"*If* I go on a date with him. I think I'll see how a telephone conversation goes first. That way I can judge for myself if he's a meathead."

"What are you waiting for? Get on the phone."

Shondra shook her head. "I don't feel like calling him back tonight. Maybe tomorrow."

"Okay, just keep me updated. Right now *your* love life is the most interesting thing I have going on."

"You'll always have the unconditional affection of your dogs."

Lisa started to walk away then turned back. "Oh, about that. I'm not working for the kennel anymore. There's only so much poop you can scoop before enough is enough."

"I heard that," Shondra agreed. "But what are you going to do now? Have you decided to go back to law?"

"Nope. I got a job in a coffee shop. I'm a barista. You can look forward to all the low-fat, caramel-mocha lattes you can handle."

"Okay. Now that sounds like a fair trade. It beats the heck out of all the unexpected piles of crap I can handle."

Connor waited outside his father's office Wednesday morning feeling more nervous than he had in a long time. He'd give anything in the world to be somewhere else at that moment.

But this morning he'd awakened with a new resolve. The only way to fight blackmail was to disarm the blackmailer. He had to tell his father what was going on. Connor was certain Carl Stewart would find some way to make this his fault, but the important thing was that he didn't allow Valerie to trap him into marriage.

Especially when he could tell it wasn't what she really wanted herself. Valerie's parting words yesterday afternoon had been very revealing. In all the years they'd known each other, she'd never cared one way or the other about love. The fact that she'd developed a bitter cynicism about it meant that she'd thought she'd found it. As hard as it was to buy that Alejandro the Latin exotic dancer was the love of her life, Connor believed it.

That's why he didn't feel the least bit guilty about taking over the situation. He'd made the first appointment of the day to see his father. It was time to make this all go away.

Finally, at 8:00 a.m. on the dot, his father opened his office door. "Good morning, Connor. Come in."

"Good morning." Connor felt beads of sweat immediately break out on his forehead. He felt like he was eight years old again. He'd disappointed his father a lot during his lifetime. But he'd spent the last few years trying to prove to him that those days of rebellion were over.

Hopefully his father would see that he was trying to be a man about this situation.

Carl settled himself behind the big oak desk that had been designed to intimidate. His large, leather wing-backed chair resembled a throne as he stared down at Connor from it. "What's on your mind, Connor?"

"I wanted to—"

"By the way, did you speak with Valerie?" Carl's brow furrowed. "What was her emergency?"

"It's interesting you should bring that up—"

"I have faith that if that woman's in trouble you'll do the right thing. My friendship with Woodrow goes back many years. I won't have anything jeopardize that. Now what was the situation?"

Before Connor realized what was happening, he'd lost his temper. "Dad, why do you always assume the worst? You're practically accusing me of knocking Valerie up."

The older man's face reddened. "There's no need for vulgar language."

Connor rolled his eyes. "Is this how little you think of me?"

"This has nothing to do with you. When I talked with Valerie, my gut instinct told me there was a serious problem she needed to discuss with you. These are the same kinds of insights I've relied on to build SI into what it is today. I have to stand behind those instincts."

Connor was on his feet, leaning across the massive desk. "Haven't I done everything in my power to prove to you that I'm responsible? Haven't I streamlined the company in the last three years to help it run more efficiently? Haven't I backed up my importance to SI with dollar signs?"

"Sit down, Connor."

Grudgingly, Connor did as his father asked.

"I've never questioned your importance to this company. You're my son. All of this will be yours one day."

"One day," he scoffed. "Why do you keep pushing back your retirement date if you don't still have reservations about my leadership?"

Carl Stewart looked away from Connor's expectant gaze. "Why don't you tell me what Valerie wanted from you?"

Connor felt himself shutting down. "It was personal. None of your concern." He stood and headed for the door.

"Connor, the one thing you still need to work on—" his father called after him "—is your temper. It takes a cool head to run Stewart Industries."

Connor stopped outside his father's closed door, with his heart sinking. Now he'd just made things worse than ever.

Shondra got into the office early that morning, hoping to devise a new plan of action for her investigation. Taking out her staff list, she decided to construct a list of people to check out. She didn't know how much information she'd be able to dig up on her own, but the Internet was a wonderful thing.

Her father had attended a lot of charity events and it would be a good start to investigate whether any SI employees had been at any of those events with her father.

Shondra was in the middle of highlighting names from different departments when Connor appeared in her doorway.

She nearly jumped out of her seat.

"Sorry, I didn't mean to scare you," he said softly.

Shondra smoothed her hand over her rapidly beating heart, while she tried to casually shift the staff list under some other paperwork on her desk.

"I didn't know anyone else was here so early." She watched his gaze drop to the hand resting on her chest, and she let it drop to her lap.

This wasn't fair. He couldn't take up with his ex-girlfriend and then stop by to stir up her day.

Connor smiled, but the wattage wasn't up to his usual standard. "I had an early meeting."

What had brought that hint of melancholy to his blue eyes? The shadows under his eyes made him look haggard. Was he having trouble sleeping at night?

Snap out of it, she ordered herself. It was no longer her place to worry about him.

"Can I help you with something?" she asked, staring down at her desk so she wouldn't stare at the man in front of her.

Connor looked over his shoulder and then stepped farther into her office. "I was just wondering if we were a bit rash in deciding not to be friends. I can't lie, Shondra. I miss you."

She missed him, too. Shondra wanted to moan

out loud with the agony of it. But she wouldn't say the words out loud. Just like that, the ice around her heart was cracking. Still, she couldn't give in, no matter how easy it would be.

"What are you proposing, Connor? That we meet for lunch and talk about our dates with other people? I think we both know that wouldn't work." Her voice came out colder than she'd intended, but it was for the best.

She wanted to press him about his dishonesty and secrets, but she didn't dare knowing she was guilty of the same. He just didn't know it yet.

And she didn't want to be around if that day ever came.

"No, I know we can't do that," he said, leaning over her desk. "But I'd like to be able to share an elevator without one of us acting like the other has the plague. I'd like to be able to joke with you over coffee in the kitchenette and get a genuine smile when we pass in the hall." He leaned closer, his eyes intense. "I just hate feeling like you hate me."

Shondra's heart melted entirely. "Connor, I don't hate you. How could I? I know this is awkward, but I don't know any way around that for now. Maybe we'll eventually get to the place where we can do some of those things you mentioned. We just have to give it time."

Connor stared at her for a minute more. In that instant she thought he might round the desk and pull her into his arms. She wouldn't have stopped him if he had.

Instead he shoved his hands into his pockets and walked out of her office.

After a few hours of trying to concentrate and failing, Shondra had to admit getting over Connor was no easy task. She had it bad, and there was only one cure for the blues over a man. Another man.

Picking up her phone, she dialed her voice mail and listened to her message from Randall Whitman. He had a deep baritone voice and good diction. She was a sucker for good diction. So far, so good. At least it seemed Randall wasn't a meathead.

She jotted down his number and dialed it from her cell phone. "Is this Randall?" she asked when the deep baritone answered the line.

"Yes, it is."

"Hi, this Shondra Braddock returning your call. I was wondering if you wanted to get together for coffee or a cocktail?" So much for seeing how the conversation went. She needed a distraction and fast.

"Make it dinner and you've got a date."

"Okay, how about this weekend?"

"Sorry, I've got to be back in Dallas for the game this weekend. How about tonight?"

Well, as far as distractions went, they didn't get any faster than that. "Okay, that sounds great. I can meet you somewhere—"

"Nonsense. I'll pick you up at eight."

"Fine," she said, giving him her address. At least he knew how to take charge.

Shondra got home from work at six-thirty knowing she only had an hour and a half before her date arrived. Yet, for some reason, she couldn't force herself to get moving. She found herself watching TV, cleaning the kitchen and checking her e-mail before she finally dragged herself into the shower.

With only fifteen minutes to spare, she pulled a comb through her hair and threw on the first outfit her fingers touched.

Despite her lack of effort, Shondra thought she'd turned out pretty well in her simple black dress and straight hair. She bent the ends up with her flat iron, and she was ready to go.

Just as she left the bedroom, Lisa called to her. "Your date just pulled up and he's driving a Lamborghini."

Shondra shrugged. "At least I think I've heard of that one."

She stood in the foyer and waited. Then thirty seconds later a loud horn sounded.

Lisa jumped up to look out the window again. "Oh no, he didn't. He's *honking* for you."

Shondra pursed her lips. "He can honk all he wants. I'm not coming out until he comes to the door."

Lisa snickered. "He's not so different from some of your old dates, after all."

Shondra marched over to the couch and joined Lisa, folding her arms stubbornly. Sure enough, after five minutes of honking, and Shondra fearing she'd be forced to move from the neighborhood, Randall finally rang the doorbell.

She walked to the door and pulled it open. "Hel—"

"What's the matter? Didn't you hear me honking?"

Shondra gave him her prettiest smile. "No,

I'm sorry. I must have been in the bedroom getting ready."

Lisa appeared behind her. "This is my room-mate, Lisa."

"Hello," Randall said, letting his eyes linger on her friend just a hair too long for her comfort. "*Very* nice to meet you."

Even Lisa seemed to pick up on his lecherous vibe because she muttered under her breath and hurried out of the room.

Trying to remain optimistic, despite all the red flags popping up, Shondra followed Randall to the car.

At least he opened her door for her. He'd had to. She hadn't been able to figure out how they worked on her own.

Randall peeled out of her drive, causing Shondra to clutch the armrest for dear life. He turned up the CD player and started cranking hard-core rap music.

"Randall… Randall? Randall!" she shouted.

He finally looked over, turning down the music so he could hear her.

"I don't really like rap music. Could we listen to some jazz or something?"

Randall frowned. "Nah, I don't like jazz. This

is Public Nuisance, baby. This is the shiznit!" He cranked up the music and Shondra's ears blistered from both the volume and the stream of curse words that flew out every other second.

It was a miserable but thankfully short drive to the restaurant he'd picked out. Shondra felt a wave of relief when they finally parked the car.

At least it was a restaurant she liked and had visited often. Maybe this date was salvageable after all.

Chapter 10

Stoically, Shondra climbed back into the car as Randall continued to rant about the restaurant from which they'd just left without eating.

"It's always been their policy to take reservations. You shouldn't take it personally—"

"Not take it personally? They acted like they didn't know who I was!" he exploded.

Oh, Lord, and she'd set him of again. Randall had made an embarrassing scene in the restaurant when they told him he needed reservations. He'd thrown his name around and had tried to bribe the maitre d', and when none of that worked, he'd started yelling.

Thanks to Randall, Shondra had now been banned from her favorite restaurant.

They finally ended up at a chain steakhouse. It had taken all of Shondra's inner fortitude not to make him turn around and take her back home. She'd promised her brothers and herself that she was going to give this date a fair shot.

But she didn't need to get to the end of the evening to know this guy wasn't for her. Randall was a glaring opposite of Connor in every way imaginable and, much to her chagrin, Shondra had found herself longing for Connor's laid-back demeanor and his sexy wicked grin.

Once they were seated in the restaurant, Randall's face seemed to have taken on a permanent scowl. It wasn't until a huge slab of prime rib was placed in front of him that he finally started to smile.

Clearly he'd been in his own world when Shondra had placed her order, because now he glared at her grilled chicken salad.

"You ordered salad in a steakhouse? Girl, that's blasphemous."

"I don't usually eat red meat, so—"

"Oh damn, I'm on a date with one of those lettuce-eating tree-hugger types. Don't you know that if God didn't want us to eat animals, he wouldn't have made them out of meat?"

"It's not that. I—"

Randall sliced into his steak and waved a rare piece of meat in front of her nose. "Smell that? That's man food right there."

Then he yanked his arm back and stuck the fork in his mouth, chewing noisily. "Mmm, mmm, mmm. There's no way your rabbit feed compares to that."

Shondra rolled her eyes and counted to ten, cursing her proper upbringing. Right then she wished she were more the outspoken type that could wave her finger in his face and give him the cussing out that he truly had coming.

Instead, because she knew anything she did could get back to her brother Malcolm, and therefore, haunt her forever, she racked her brain for a way to change the subject.

Shondra didn't know a thing about football, since basketball was more her game, but she knew the safest topic of conversation would be Randall himself. "How long have you been with the Dallas Cowboys?"

Randall talked about his football career and all the perks being a pro athlete had brought him. She learned about his six cars in detail, as well as his vacation home in Miami and his custom-tailored designer clothes.

And when he was done with that, he finally asked Shondra about herself. She kept it simple, hitting the highlights of her job and interests, and to her surprise, they discovered they both loved the stock market. They discussed their investment preferences and, by dessert, the two of them finally seemed to be getting along.

As they walked out to the parking lot, Randall started pointing out the features of his black Lamborghini.

Since they'd reached a friendly space, Shondra decided to test the waters. "Can I drive it?"

Randall stopped in his tracks and stared at her. "Girl, are you crazy? This a $350,000 car. Hell no, you can't drive it."

Shondra rolled her eyes and got into the car. Why wasn't she surprised?

When the car finally pulled into her driveway, Shondra had her feet on the pavement before he could turn off the engine. "Good night," she called over her shoulder, and jogged to the door.

She pretended not to hear him calling for her to wait. She unlocked the door like she had a serial killer on her heels and slammed it shut behind her.

Malcolm had some explaining to do.

Shondra was tired when she got into the office the next morning. Missing a little sleep wasn't a problem when there had been a good time to justify it. But, after her date last night, Shondra knew she'd been better off on her own.

She hadn't been in her chair for more than five minutes when her cell phone rang. "Hello?"

"How did your date go?"

Shondra rolled her eyes. "Malcolm, you must have been out of your mind to set me up with a meathead like that."

"Why? He seemed like a great guy when I met him."

"He's arrogant, selfish, rude—it was the worst date of my life. He even got me banned from my favorite restaurant."

"You're kidding."

"I wish I was. It was a nightmare. I tried it your way and it was a disaster. So, I don't ever want to hear another word about you setting me up on a blind date ever again."

Shondra caught a movement from the corner of her eye and saw Connor standing in her doorway. "I have to get back to work, Malcolm. I'll talk to you later," she said, hanging up the phone.

Connor's face had taken on a slightly pinker tinge than normal. "You went on a blind date last night? With who?"

The words *none of your business* were on the tip of her tongue, but the hurt expression on his face held them back. "A friend of my brother's. It wasn't a big deal."

Connor nodded, perking up a tiny bit as he teased, "I believe your exact word was *disaster.*"

Shondra wrinkled her brow. "Why were you eavesdropping on my conversation?"

"I didn't intend to. I came to your office to get your signature on these contracts."

She looked over the stack of forms in his hand. "You could have sent those through interoffice mail."

"I want them signed right away. I can't help that you were taking a personal call on company time." His eyes sparkled with good humor and Shondra felt her heart do a little flip in her chest.

Uh-oh, she was headed for trouble again. Forcing an edge into her voice, Shondra said,

"I'm sorry about that. Sarah said she saw you visiting with your ex-girlfriend the other day. I suppose *that* was business?"

As soon as the words were out of her mouth, Shondra regretted them. Now she sounded like a jealous shrew. What's more, her careless words could get Sarah in trouble.

Connor's expression blanked. "She just wanted to ask a favor."

"It's none of my business either way," Shondra said, looking away now that the moment had gone sour.

Connor crossed over to her and laid the contracts on her desk. When he didn't say anything more, she was forced to look up.

He was watching her with a pained look. An ache from deep inside her mirrored his expression. Neither one of them said anything.

"Get these back to me as soon as you can," he said, finally turning to leave.

When he was out of sight, Shondra slumped in her chair. How had they gotten to this awkward place? It had only been one weekend. And then she remembered.

Connor was being blackmailed. And it seemed to be taking its toll on him. Was he all right?

She called herself a fool for letting herself worry about him. She still cared about Connor, but there wasn't room in her life for her problems and his.

Before she could finish that train of thought, the phone on her desk rang. "Shondra Braddock speaking."

"Back off, bitch," said a muffled female voice, then the line went dead.

Chapter 11

Later that afternoon, Shondra rode the elevator up to Carl Stewart's office. This had not been a good day. In fact, it hadn't been a good week.

Her prank phone call had been followed by three others that were exactly the same. Her nerves were so rattled, she'd actually headed down to the HR department to report the harassment. They might be able to trace the calls if they were coming from inside the building.

But halfway to the department, Shondra had turned back. She couldn't report the note and the phone calls, and she didn't have any proof that her car accident had been related. No one would be able to help her unless she was ready to explain exactly what she'd been doing at Stewart Industries.

Since she wasn't ready to do that, she had to sit on her hands a little longer.

When Carl's assistant directed her to enter his office, Shondra's heart started racing out of control. She didn't know what he could possibly need, but the way the rest of her day was going, she felt that it wasn't going to be good.

The older Stewart made an imposing figure, peering down at her from behind his big oak desk. "Close the door behind you, please, Shondra."

She did as he asked and sat in one of the guest chairs in front of him.

"You're probably wondering why I called you here today."

"Yes, as a matter of fact, I am."

"This is a delicate subject. I don't usually like to get involved in the personal lives of my employees. But the circumstances here are unique."

Shondra bit her lower lip. This involved her personal life? That could only mean—

"Shondra, I know that you've been seeing my son…socially."

She felt her cheeks blazing with heat. If she could melt into a little puddle and seep out the door, she would have. This was her worst-case scenario. "It's true that we have spent time together…socially, but we've ended things."

Carl studied her for a moment, during which Shondra could feel herself breaking into a sweat. If he fired her, it would almost be a relief. But she didn't want to end her time there as a failure.

"I can't deny that I'm glad to hear that, Shondra. It's nothing personal, but Connor is going to become CEO of Stewart Industries one day. He can't afford any distractions right now. I'd be having this conversation with him, instead of you. But you know my son. Telling him not to do something is the same as giving him an engraved invitation."

Shondra swallowed, feeling more uncomfortable by the minute. "Yes, well, if that's all you wanted to discuss—"

"You must be wondering how I found out about the two of you."

She watched him, awaiting his answer.

"I've noticed Connor has been preoccupied lately. So I took it upon myself to check into his weekend excursion to Monte Carlo. The pilot was able to confirm that you were the other passenger on the company jet."

Shondra nodded, unsure what to say. She felt like she was sitting there naked. He knew more about her love life than she wanted him to.

"I don't want to pry," Carl started, indicating that he fully intended to do just that. "But I need to know, which one of you broke things off."

"Um, I did."

Carl nodded. "I see. Well, I think we both know that Connor can be quite stubborn when it comes to things that he wants. He doesn't usually take no for an answer. That can be useful in business, but in this case, it could be a problem. I'm sure I don't have to tell you to resist any of his further advances."

Shondra felt her body going cold. It was one thing to discuss violating a company policy regarding fraternization; it was another to be told whom she could or could not date. She wasn't aware of any formal policies, so it was possible that intimidation was Carl's only course of action.

Suddenly, Shondra was reminded of her father. She had a little bit of insight to the kind of family pressure that Connor often rebelled against. He was bolder in his rebellions than she had been.

In any case, Shondra couldn't sit still for his intimate probing any longer. She rose to her feet. "Carl, you can rest assured that if your son makes any further advances toward me, I will handle it as I see fit."

Shondra walked out of Carl Stewart's office quickly, as though she was expecting a bullet in her back. Thankfully, that bullet never came.

Connor smiled when Shondra appeared in his doorway, holding the contracts he'd left with her earlier. Interoffice mail worked both ways. Apparently she couldn't stay away, just as he hadn't been able to.

His expression changed when he noted the tight set of her mouth. "What's wrong?" he asked as she handed him the paperwork.

She leaned forward so her voice wouldn't carry out the door. He could smell the subtle fragrance of gardenia she sometimes wore. "I had a *lovely* conversation with your father today."

Connor's spine snapped straight. Her sarcasm told him that it hadn't been about business. "Close the door."

When she crossed back over to his desk, he asked, "What did he say?"

"That he knows we were in Monte Carlo together."

Connor slumped in his seat. "And what did you say?"

"I told him that things were over between us, and believe me, he was thrilled to hear that."

Connor swore viciously. He started to rise to his feet but Shondra stopped him.

"Don't you dare. You look like you're about to go running out of here to confront him, and trust me, I've had enough humiliation for one day."

"Shondra, I can't let him—"

"I'm serious. The only reason I'm telling you about this is to make sure you realize that there's no going back. I got the feeling this morning that you might be hoping for…something. And now that your father knows, it's really important that we don't have anything to do with each other."

Connor's eyes went icy cold. "Did he threaten you?"

"No, of course not. He was very respectful considering the uncomfortable circumstances. I'm not asking to please him. I'm talking to you because I want you to spare me any further embarrassment by making this any worse. Can you do that much for me?"

Connor looked at Shondra. She looked beautiful and all he really wanted was to pull her across the desk into his arms. But that was off-limits. More than ever now.

She wanted him to protect her. Every instinct in his body told him to go to his father's office and ream him out for interfering in his personal life. But doing that would only serve to hurt Shondra.

That was the last thing he wanted.

"Okay, Shondra. I'll let it go."

"Thank you," she said softly before leaving his office.

Connor sat there staring at the contracts on his desk without really seeing them. He'd never felt more out of control of his life than he did right then.

Valerie had made it clear that she'd be showing up tomorrow to find out his answer. He couldn't marry her. Of course, as soon as his father found out, he would try to force the issue. Connor didn't have any doubt that he'd hold the company over him to make him marry Valerie.

Connor laid his head in his hands. He had no idea what he was going to do.

When Shondra returned to her office that evening, she found an interoffice mail envelope on her chair. Still shaken up from the barrage of crank phone calls that afternoon, she wasn't sure what she could expect to find when she opened it. It was a brand-new envelope with no names listed in the To or From columns.

She'd just picked up the envelope when Diane, the office assistant, appeared in her doorway. Forcing herself to pull it together, Shondra dropped the envelope and turned to face the woman.

"Do you need something, Diane?"

Nodding, she approached Shondra's desk, holding out a brochure. Judging by the timid expression on the other woman's face, Shondra knew she wasn't doing a good enough job of hiding her own fluster.

"Uh, yes, I just found these. They are travel plans for a seminar in Vegas that Charlie Howard had made before he left SI. I was wondering if you wanted me to convert the reservations into your name?"

Shondra blinked. A seminar in Las Vegas? She was pretty sure she didn't have time for anything like that. "When is the seminar?"

"Monday."

Shondra shook her head. "I don't think I'm

going to go, Diane. But why don't you leave the information here, and I'll make a decision once I've had a chance to look over the materials."

Diane dropped the pamphlet on her desk and hurried out of the room, finally giving Shondra the opportunity to open the envelope.

Holding her breath, Shondra reached inside and pulled out a sheet of paper. Typed in the middle of the document in a nondescript font were the words: "Harmon Braddock was murdered. Don't stop looking for answers."

Shondra felt like a thief in the night. Literally. It was seven o'clock on Saturday night and she was breaking into Stewart Industries.

Actually, she had a key, so there wasn't any breaking and entering involved. But she had definite plans to go where she didn't belong. And her first stop was Connor's office.

Extreme times called for extreme measures. And Shondra wasn't ready for her life to get any more out of control. This had been a particularly tough week. It was time for her to put her life back in order. That meant getting whatever information she could and leaving Stewart Industries as soon as possible.

Now she knew there were two forces at work at SI. Someone who wanted her to back off the investigation, and someone who wanted her to keep looking for answers. Shondra couldn't waste any time waiting to see whose tactics would prove most aggressive. She had to make her move.

Shondra knew the office building would be empty this late on a Saturday evening. Even the dedicated brown-nosers would have packed up and headed home by now.

As Shondra walked down the empty dim-lit halls, she couldn't help noticing how eerie it was in there. Considering the threatening note and crank calls she'd been receiving, Shondra realized she didn't want to hang around any longer than necessary.

Quickly slipping into Connor's office, Shondra sat at his desk. As many times as she'd been in this office in the past, for some reason, seeing it when she wasn't supposed to be here was different. Suddenly she noticed things she'd been too distracted to notice when Connor had been with her.

Reaching out, she picked up the picture on Connor's desk. His mother. She had given her son her ice-blue eyes and flaxen blond hair. It was no surprise that she was a beautiful woman. Shondra had suspected as much. But the picture *did* surprise her.

It wasn't the kind of formally posed portrait that many people would keep on a desk. This was a moment frozen in time. A moment captured when Connor's mother was young and healthy. She was wearing a bathrobe and her hair was mussed, and in her arms she cradled a toddler who had just dribbled food on her collar.

Shondra felt tears welling in her eyes. She learned so much about Connor from this photo on his desk. And her heart ached.

Shaking it off, Shondra put the picture back where she found it. This wasn't the time to moon over Connor. That ship had sailed. Especially now that the senior Stewart had found out about them. But she had to admit, there was now a bit of a Romeo and Juliet syndrome in effect. It was one thing when their breakup had been her idea. Now that Daddy Stewart had made it official, thinking about Connor was all Shondra had been able to do.

Right then, her gaze fell on a CD case lying on his desk. The Dixie Chicks. Apparently he'd been giving country music a try. A knot rose in her throat. She'd had an impact on Connor's life. Maybe their time together hadn't been a simple fling to Connor. He'd cared enough about the music she liked to try to acquire an appreciation for it himself.

Shondra pressed her eyes closed. She had to get this over with and get out. She was supposed to be putting Connor out of her life. The longer she sat in his environment, smelled his cologne in the air and touched his trinkets, the more she wished things had been different....

Shondra forced her attention to the task at hand—raiding Connor's office for information. She was relieved to see that he had left his computer logged on. That would save her from going through his filing cabinets. She knew he had access to all the drives on the company's system.

All she had to do was to figure out where the phone logs were kept and she'd know who her father had been contacting at SI.

She was just starting to make some progress when she heard the elevator door down the hall open.

Shondra's heartbeat started hammering in her chest as the footsteps headed in her direction. Swallowing hard, she started closing files. She barely got the computer monitor turned off before a tired-looking Connor appeared in the doorway.

He stopped in his tracks as he took her in, sitting behind his desk. "What are you doing here?"

Shondra opened her mouth, without any clue what would come out. "I wanted to leave you a note." She looked down at the desk with no pen and no pad handy. "But I wasn't sure what I wanted to say…so, I was thinking—"

Connor took a step toward her. He looked terrible and wonderful at the same time. He was wearing jeans and a long-sleeved black T-shirt that showed off the delicious muscles in his chest. But his eyes had dark circles under them and his normally perfect blond hair looked as if he'd been raking it with his fingers for hours.

"Why did you want to leave me a note?"

"The conversation we had last… Um, I just didn't like how we left things." That was true. Things had never felt so final between them until then.

At once his body seemed to relax. "God, you don't know how badly I needed to hear that."

Shondra stood. "I didn't expect anyone to be here this late. I'll get out of your way."

Connor rounded the desk, effectively blocking

her path to the door. Shondra held her breath as she raised her gaze to meet his.

In that moment she saw a mirror of all the emotions she'd been hiding from over the last week: loneliness, longing and a deep desire that had been causing her to toss and turn at night.

They stared at each other for a second, then Connor reached out and yanked her against him.

Shondra threw her arms around his neck and leaned up into his frantic kiss.

Connor's mouth moved quickly over her lips and face as his hands pulled her body tightly to his. She felt as if she were caught up in a tornado that was going to spin her into the unknown.

Part of her wanted to just let herself be blown away without concern for where she would land. But another part of her couldn't do it.

Pulling away, she looked up into Connor's face. "Wait a minute. What are we doing?"

He gripped her waist and set her on the edge of his desk. "Putting ourselves out of our misery," he said, stepping between her legs and pressing his mouth over hers once again.

Shondra leaned away from his kisses. "Yes, but we said we wouldn't—"

His hands slipped up her jeans to the hem of

her T-shirt. Connor pushed her hair away from her neck and she could feel his breath against her skin. "Do you want me to stop?" he asked right against her ear.

Shondra realized both of her hands were flat against Connor's rear end. Her life had been hanging upside down the entire week. In that moment, for the first time, things felt right.

"No. Don't stop."

Connor began trailing kisses down her neck, and she squeezed a handful of rock-hard flesh. Then they were kissing again.

Things were rolling off the desk as he leaned into her, pressing her farther back onto the desk.

"Ouch," she shrieked as something stabbed her in the thigh.

Connor pulled away, looking down at her with a heavy-lidded gaze. "What's wrong?"

Shondra shifted uncomfortably. "This type of scene always plays better in romance novels."

Connor pulled her off the desk and half carried her to the sofa, settling her on his lap. Shondra could feel every inch of his erection.

Before she could react, he'd tugged her shirt over her head. He raked his fingers down her back, raising goose bumps all over her skin.

She immediately began tugging at Connor's shirt. The second her fingers found the velvety skin over his muscles she moaned with pleasure.

She was so enraptured with the rippling sight of his pectorals and biceps that it took her a minute to realize that he'd become very still.

Looking up, she saw that Connor was staring at her like a long-lost puppy. When she met his gaze, his eyes clouded. "I've missed you so much."

Shondra's heart splintered. If she'd thought this moment was just about sex, his expression told her different. Emotion clogged her throat. No words could break through.

She was so relieved when Connor pushed her to her feet so he could unfasten her jeans. While she tugged them down her legs, he was working on removing his own pants and underwear.

When they were both naked, Connor had her in his arms again. He held her close, kissing her, and letting his hands find every sensitive spot from her lower back to her neck. When he'd brought her to a near frenzy of sensation, he guided her back to the couch.

Shondra was surprised when he didn't lay her on her back or pull her onto his lap. Instead he positioned her on her knees on the cushions, leaning her over the armrest.

She began to smile with pleasure as he stroked her feminine folds, making sure she was ready for him. Finally, when Shondra thought that she would go out of her mind from his touch, he pulled out a condom.

Connor stretched one masculine arm around her body to stimulate her as he entered her from behind. She felt a new thrill of excitement as she felt his chest against her back.

Their bodies came together at a frenzied pace. Their pent-up passion pushed them into a hurried rhythm that sent them over the edge in just a few strokes.

Shondra cried out and felt Connor's answering groan as he collapsed, chest heaving against her back. Gently pulling out from her, Connor fell back against the cushions, taking Shondra with him.

They lay that way for several minutes, letting the air cool their perspiring bodies. As her heartbeat returned to normal, Shondra realized that she'd managed to do what had just that morning seem impossible.

She'd made her complicated life…even more complicated.

Chapter 12

Connor lay against the cushions on the sofa, feeling a sense of peace he hadn't felt in many days. But he knew that peace of mind was tenuous. Shondra hadn't spoken a word in the last few minutes.

Finally she sat up and reached for her bra. Connor took her arm and gently pulled her back against his chest, trying to prolong the moment. He knew that thin barrier of cotton between them would become a cement wall. She'd be closed off from him again.

He smoothed her hair away from her ear and

whispered, "Why don't you come back to my apartment? I'll make you some dinner and we can talk."

He felt her body go rigid in his arms. He closed his eyes, waiting for the other shoe to drop.

Shondra sighed heavily as she pulled forward out of his reach. He watched her scoot to the far side of the sofa, balling herself up to hug her knees. Then she raised her gaze to his. "Connor—"

He knew all she had to say from her tone of voice. Deciding to rip off the Band-Aid quickly, he reached out and handed Shondra her clothes. "I know what you're going to say. Nothing's changed, right?"

She held her T-shirt up to her chest like a shield of armor. "Has it? Has your life become any less complicated?"

Connor paused to study her as he tugged on his jeans. Did she know about Valerie? He fastened the snap and sat back down on the sofa. Even if she didn't know anything about what he'd been dealing with over the past week, her point was well taken.

"Because nothing in *my* life has simplified," she said. "We can't do anything like this again. It just makes things harder. You know I have strong feelings for you, but I can't take the time to wade through them right now."

She busied herself putting on her clothes, and Connor stayed silent. Things might be more complicated, but how could he walk away from the one person who made him feel good? Connor felt like he'd been flying around in the winds of a tornado and, on that sofa, he'd finally found the calm center. The ferocious winds were still whirring around them, but he didn't want to leave the safety of her arms.

"I understand everything you're saying, but I just can't get past the fact that we really have something. It's more than just an affair. Even if things are complicated, I think it's worth fighting for."

Shondra was dressed now, and she stopped and stared at him. He could see the longing in her face. For a second he felt himself holding his breath. Was there any chance of her giving in?

Instead she rubbed both of her hands over her face, shaking her head. "I wish. Connor, I really wish I could."

Then she walked out of the office without looking back, leaving Connor once again.

* * *

It was all Shondra could do not to collapse in the elevator. The weight of this week's events was crushing her. Why couldn't she just run away from it all? She wanted to forget about her father's death and her responsibilities to her family.

She'd give anything to be back in Monte Carlo with Connor. Shondra wished she could stop time and trap them in those moments forever. But that wasn't possible and the real world had more than caught up with them.

She knew for a fact someone at Stewart Industries knew about her father's death. No matter how much she might want to, she couldn't run away from that. But there was definitely more at stake than ever. After the threats and her car accident, she just couldn't be too careful.

With that on her mind, she had the office building's security officer walk her to her car in the garage. And as she drove home, she made a decision.

She couldn't run away forever, but it wouldn't hurt to leave town for a few days. She still had a chance to attend that seminar in Las Vegas. A change of scenery could help her clear her head.

When Shondra walked into her condo, Lisa was waiting for her. She jumped up from the sofa and ran to meet her. "What's going on?"

Shondra stared at her friend. "I was just about to ask you the same thing. You look frantic."

"I am. Have you checked the answering machine lately? It's filled with messages from some lunatic girl warning you to stay away from her man. 'Back off, bitch' and all sorts of nonsense like that."

Shondra's body went cold. "What are you talking about?"

Lisa pointed to the phone on the wall in the front hall. "Go on, check the voice mail yourself."

Shondra dialed into the voice-mail system and it told her there were seven saved messages. They were all from the same woman telling her to stay away from Connor, the father of her baby.

Feeling her entire body going numb, she hung up the phone and stared at Lisa. "Oh my God" was the only thing she could say.

Lisa dragged her into the kitchen and sat her down at the kitchen table. "As soon as I heard the messages, I went to the grocery store." Shondra looked over the plate of spicy chicken empanadas with pleasure.

In times of crisis, Shondra didn't turn to ice cream or chocolate. Her comfort food of choice was the meat-filled pastry Lisa had introduced her to in college. The recipe had come straight from Lisa's Jamaican grandmother. When Shondra learned of her father's death, Lisa had prepared them every night for a week.

Shondra picked one up and bit into it with gusto. "Mmm. I've been eating a lot of these lately. If my life doesn't start getting better, I'm going to be very fat."

"You and me both," Lisa said, picking one out for herself. "So, do you know who this woman is? And did Connor really get her pregnant?"

Shondra sighed as the pieces began to fall into place. "I'm starting to figure this out." She wasn't being stalked by someone who knew she was investigating her father's death. She was being harassed by Connor's girlfriend, Valerie.

Lisa shook her head. "You've had a lot on your mind. Do you want to tell me about it?"

Shondra realized she had been holding a lot in. It wasn't like her not to confide in her best friend. "Yes."

And over that plate of empanadas she told Lisa about the anonymous call that placed her at Stewart Industries, the conversation she overheard in Monte Carlo and the messages that she now realized had been from Valerie.

She thought about just how close she'd been to throwing in with Connor again. In fact, she'd just spent the evening in his arms.

What a fool she'd been.

Connor came into the office Monday morning with new resolve. He couldn't look at his sofa without thinking of Shondra. He knew he had to do whatever it took to convince her to take a chance on their relationship.

He'd avoided Valerie's calls all weekend and had slept on an old fraternity buddy's couch so he wouldn't be around if she showed up unexpectedly. He planned to take care of his problems with her on his own terms. And this morning, the private investigator he'd hired told him exactly where Alejandro had been hiding.

He'd just picked up the phone to dial her number when she came strutting through his office door. "Where have you been all weekend?"

Connor rolled his eyes. "That's none of your business. Close the door. I want to talk to you."

Valerie slammed the door. "I hope you spent your weekend at some exclusive resort with your black Barbie doll because after she gets my messages she's not going to want to have anything to do with you."

Connor felt his composure slip to his feet. "Messages? What are you talking about?"

"That's right. I told you there would be consequences. Obviously you were still holding out some kind of hope of getting back together with her. I've just made things a lot easier for you."

He was on his feet in a flash. "Valerie, what did you do?"

"I told your little friend to stay away from my baby's daddy."

Connor collapsed into his chair swearing viciously.

"Now, now, Connor," Valerie said, holding her stomach. "You don't want our child to hear such language."

Breathing deeply, he tried to rein in his temper. Maybe she was just goading him. "How did you get Shondra's number?"

Valerie laughed, making herself comfortable

on the very couch where Connor had last made love to Shondra. "You're not the only one who can hire a private investigator."

Connor froze.

"That's right. I know that you've been checking up on me. What? Did you think I wouldn't find out that your man for hire was going around questioning my friends? Were you trying to find something to blackmail me with?"

"No. I was trying to find Alejandro. And I did. That's why I wanted to talk to you."

Valerie's face changed immediately. "You found him?" In a flash, she'd gone from manipulative bitch to lovelorn girl.

Yeah, Connor thought bitterly, he knew that expression. She had it bad. It took one to know one. "Yes, I found him."

"What did he say?"

Connor shook his head. "First tell me everything you said to Shondra."

Valerie had the decency to blush as she confessed the contents of her note, messages and to accidently rear-ending Shondra's car.

Connor raked his hands over his face. This mess hadn't just blown up in *his* face. It had exploded all over Shondra. No wonder her nerves had been stretched thin.

He pinned Valerie with a deadly look. "I've got some good news about Alejandro, but before I give it to you, you have to promise to help me fix this mess you've gotten me into with Shondra."

As Shondra rode the elevator to her room in Las Vegas's Bellagio hotel, she couldn't help feeling like a coward. She'd literally run away from her problems.

Sure she could spend the next two days sitting in a seminar that would update her on the latest in risk management and compliance, and that could make her better at her job down the road. But it wasn't going to improve anything relevant to her life right now.

The man she'd been sleeping with had gotten his ex-girlfriend pregnant, and the woman was probably trying to trap him into marriage. And all the while he was still trying to convince *her* that they had a future together.

Yeah right.

Meanwhile, this crazy woman had been harassing her with phone calls and nasty sticky notes. All of which was a distraction from the real issue in her life. Someone at Stewart Industries knew that her father's death wasn't an accident. That person had tried to contact her.

She was on the right track for the first time in weeks and instead of running down that lead, she was in Las Vegas. Maybe her brothers had been right. Maybe she was in this over her head.

Right now, Shondra was hiding from her feelings of hurt and betrayal. Why did it seem that a woman's downfall was always at the hands of a man? She couldn't let that happen to her.

Pulling her rolling case into her room, Shondra noticed that her message light was already blinking. She hoped it wasn't Connor. Because he was her boss, he had access to her whereabouts, but if he knew what was good for him, he'd give her a wide berth right now.

To her relief, it was a message from the conference director telling her she was signed up as a volunteer and should attend a mandatory orientation meeting in Suite 1205 at two. According to her watch, Shondra would barely have twenty minutes to freshen up.

Since the conference registration was second-hand, Shondra hadn't realized she would be expected to participate as a volunteer, but she figured it would be a good distraction.

Changing out of the track suit she'd worn to travel in, she put on a pair of slacks and a light-weight sweater. She freshened up her makeup and then headed up to Suite 1205.

She was in the midst of mentally speculating on her possible duties when Connor Stewart opened the suite door.

Staring up into his face, her jaw fell open. Before she could spin on her heel and leave, Connor pulled her into the room.

"Don't run away. We have some things to clear up."

Shondra was about to start arguing, but she noticed that they weren't the only two people in the room. A bleached blonde and handsome Latin American man were perched on the sofa.

"What's going on here?"

"Shondra, this is my ex-girlfriend, Valerie, and her fiancé, Alejandro."

Shondra cut her eyes at him. "What are you doing? Trying to pawn your baby's mother off on someone else, then convince me that the coast is clear for the two of us?"

Valerie stood and walked up to Shondra. "I

owe you an apology. All of this isn't Connor's fault. Alejandro is the father of my child. I only said it was Connor's so that he would marry me and keep my father from disinheriting me." She turned to Alejandro, who was staring up at her lovingly. "I thought Alejandro had abandoned me. That my father had paid him off. I didn't look for him myself because I didn't want a man who couldn't stand up to my father. It turns out he's renting his apartment and working two jobs to try to prove to my father that he'll make a good husband and father."

Shondra surveyed the woman with disbelief. "You mean to tell me that you've been calling my house and leaving me nasty notes, and I'm just supposed to accept your apology? You were trying to trap Connor into marriage and making my life miserable in the process."

The woman nodded, looking genuinely remorseful. "It's worse than that. I rear-ended your car."

"That was you?" Shondra's entire body went white-hot with anger. "You're the hit-and-run driver? You've been stalking me!"

Valerie bowed her head. "I'll pay for your car. Hell, I'll pay for your first child's college education. I just want to wipe the slate clean. Now that I've seen what Alejandro is willing to do to be with me, I want to make a fresh start. I want to be a better person and set a good example for our baby."

Shondra rolled her eyes. She had no desire to look at the woman any longer. Connor must have picked up on that vibe because he hustled Valerie and her fiancé out of the room.

He came back and sat beside her on the sofa. Her head was spinning. Just minutes ago, in her mind, Connor was a louse. Now he was back to the man she…loved?

"Now it's just you and me. I know you're going to accuse me of stalking you. But when I found out what Valerie had done, I knew I couldn't let you go on thinking that I'd two-timed you or had gotten some other woman pregnant."

Shondra leaned back. "I can't tell you how relieved I am to hear this." She rubbed her temple. "So is Valerie the person you accused of blackmailing you when I heard you on the phone in Monte Carlo?"

He paled. "You heard that? And all this time…" He ran his hands through his hair. "I guess that explains why you wanted to leave so suddenly. Yes, it was Valerie I was talking to."

Shondra studied him. "She's a real piece of work. So that's your type, huh?"

"No. You're my type. Valerie is someone I used to have things in common with. We outgrew each other a long time ago."

She smiled shyly. "Good. I was starting to question your taste."

Connor didn't fall into banter with her. Instead his expression became very serious. "Listen. I've heard all the arguments against us. I know your life is still complicated. But Saturday you asked me if my life had gotten any easier and as of today it has."

"Connor—"

"No, just hear me out. What that means is that I can be here for you. As much or as little as you need. I just don't want to be cut out of your life entirely. You're scheduled to be here in Las Vegas for the next three days. Just spend some of that time with me. If at the end of those three days, you really believe we don't have a chance at something real, then I'll accept your decision. I just can't let you go. Not that easily."

Shondra's heart felt amazingly light. Knowing what Connor had been struggling with for the past week had changed everything. At least as far as she was concerned. But that didn't change things in her life.

None of that really mattered at the moment. She had another chance to spend time with Connor and nothing was going to stand in their way. If everything went the way she hoped, at the end of those three days, she'd lay her cards on the table.

Then they could start fresh.

Chapter 13

Running away from home was the best decision Shondra could have made, she thought when she awoke the next morning. She'd decided not to register for the conference and had checked out of her room. Now ensconced in Connor's suite, she wanted to enjoy this brief reprieve from the drama in their lives.

"I saw the country music album on your desk when I was in your office last weekend," Shondra told him as she stretched out on his bed.

They'd spent the evening making love and had ordered room service for dinner. Shondra wouldn't have been opposed to spending another day in the suite, but she had a feeling Connor would want to take advantage of the pleasures Las Vegas had to offer.

He crossed the room, wearing nothing but his black boxer-briefs. Shondra had a great appreciation for the fact that when they were together, they often wore nothing more than their underwear. And not even that for long. "You caught me. I've been giving it a try. How about you? How is your hip-hop education coming along?"

"I'm afraid I'd receive a failing grade, Professor."

Connor lay beside her on the bed. "Oh no, we're going to have to do something about that. This afternoon, we're going to hit a record store and buy you the essentials. Dr. Dre, Jay-Z, 2-Pac, Wu-Tang…. Study them well. There will be a test."

Shondra giggled. "A test? On what? I don't even think I can remember half of those names you just mentioned. Is there a study guide?"

Connor rubbed his chin with mock seriousness. "The material covered on the test will focus primarily on vocabulary. For instance, what does *getting crunked* mean?"

Shondra narrowed her eyes trying to come up with a reasonable guess. "Um, getting drunk?"

"Nope. It means getting hyped up. Having a good time."

She frowned. "Well, I never would have guessed from the way the word sounded."

Connor nodded. "That's why you're going to need to study hard."

Shondra measured the wicked gleam in his ice-blue eyes. "And what happens if I fail the test?"

"You don't want to fail the test. There will be grave consequences."

"Like what? I hope you don't mean something like withholding sex. I'm pretty sure I can hold out longer than you can."

"Agreed. No, this is not a punishment for me. It will be a punishment for you."

Shondra propped herself up on one arm, regarding him with confidence. "I'm sure I can handle anything you dish out."

"Oh yeah. I seem to remember that you're very ticklish. Care to deny it?"

She backed away from him on the bed. "No and I haven't failed the test yet. So don't go getting any ideas—"

He advanced on her. "It seems to me you're

going to need a preview to properly motivate you in your studies."

Shondra jumped up to her feet and leaped off the bed. Connor was after her in a flash but she managed to slip through his grasp by a hair. Rounding the bed, she ran into the dining area.

Connor was quick on his feet and cornered her behind the round dining room table. She feigned right and ran left, getting around the table just before he could grab her.

"You may as well surrender because you know I'll catch you eventually."

"Don't be so sure," she called, leaping over the sofa and running around the coffee table.

He chased her in a circle and she found herself short of breath. "I am sure. Your only hope is to run into the hall. And I know you're too modest to go out there in nothing but your underwear."

Processing this truth as she ran into the foyer, she had the dubious choice of being trapped in the powder room or the wet bar. But she was the competitive type and didn't want to give in easily.

Making a quick loop around him, she poured her last thread of energy into running ahead of him into the bedroom.

She ducked behind the door, and as he came

running in full speed past her, she tackled him. "I win," she shouted, trying to dig her fingers into the hard muscles below his ribs.

Connor lay back on the carpet, panting from their exertion. Tucking his hands behind his head, he laughed at her. "I'm not ticklish."

Nevertheless, Shondra persisted in trying to find some give in his tightly muscled body. "I don't believe you."

She wiggled her fingers up his sides to his armpits and he just regarded her with mild amusement. She tucked her fingers under his back and tried to probe his butt cheeks for a ticklish spot to no avail.

When the vigorous tickling proved fruitless, Shondra changed her tactic. Trailing her fingers over his nipples with a feather's lightness, she began to explore his body. Although he tried to keep his expression blank, she saw an immediate response as he began to squirm beneath her.

"Stop that," he finally said, trying to grab her fingers.

She giggled. "I thought you weren't ticklish."

"I'm not," he said breathlessly. "That's cheating."

She evaded his swatting hands and continued her tender assault on his torso.

When he'd had enough of her exquisite torture, he gripped her by the waist and rolled her beneath him. Shondra braced herself for a defensive tickling attack that never came.

Instead she became immediately aware of his arousal. As he dropped his mouth down on hers, he pinned her arms above her head.

Within minutes he'd removed their underwear and was driving into her with a leisurely grace. He held Shondra's wrists above her head with one hand and her raised leg in the other. As he ground his pelvis into hers, Connor held her with his intense blue gaze.

Breathless, gasping for air, Shondra wanted to close her eyes. But she couldn't. The intimate connection with Connor's eyes was too powerful for her to turn away from.

Suddenly, before she was ready for it to end, something inside her uncoiled and her head fell back. But before she could register the loss, Connor released her limbs and curled against her.

Lifting his head over hers, he reestablished their connection. Connor smiled down at her tenderly and Shondra felt complete.

* * *

After dressing, Connor had insisted on taking her to his favorite all-you-can-eat buffet off the strip. When Shondra had jokingly said that she didn't think those were meant for billionaires like himself, he'd responded that billionaires liked bargains, too. Shondra had laughed heartily, because she was sure that was true.

During their time in Las Vegas, Shondra began to get to know Connor in a way she never had before. She already knew the powerful businessman who managed his employees with loyalty and compassion. And she knew the flashy playboy who'd whisked her off to Monte Carlo for luxury and romance. But she was starting to finally get to know Connor.

The man who couldn't get his day started without a diet soda. The closet techno geek who became giddy over portable hard drives and PDA software. And most recently, Shondra discovered the man who covered his plate when he was finished eating.

"Why do you do that?" she asked, watching as Connor dabbed at the corners of his mouth, then neatly covered his entire plate with his dark red napkin.

"Do what?" he asked, looking up at her.

She pointed at his plate. "You cover your plate almost ceremonially when you finish you food. You do it every time. Like you're laying it to rest."

Connor looked at his plate and shrugged. "I don't like to look at my empty plate. Or maybe I don't want anyone to notice what a glutton I am."

Shondra frowned at him. "You're hardly a glutton," she said, thinking of his rock-hard abs.

He leaned forward on his elbows. "You know how every parent tells their kid, 'clean your plate, there are starving children in Africa' right?"

She nodded.

"Well, I always took that to heart. I guess it's a bit of the guilt of the overprivileged. I always thought that if I didn't clean my plate I was causing children to starve in Africa. And whenever I couldn't finish something, I would cover it with my napkin so the starving children in Africa wouldn't know."

Shondra laughed. "Really?"

"Yeah, that was my ten-year-old logic, anyway. I haven't thought about that for years. But that's obviously where the habit started. It's funny because I didn't even realize that it was something I still did."

After brunch, Connor took Shondra shopping in the mall at Ceasar's Palace. Feeling over-dressed yet again in suit pants and a lightweight sweater, Shondra found herself in need of some-thing more casual.

"This is the second time I've packed for a business trip and found myself in leisure wear. From now on, I'm going to have to overpack for so-called business trips at Stewart Industries," Shondra said, walking out of a store with two pairs of jeans and some causal tops.

Connor slipped his arm around her waist as they walked into the bustling mall crowd. "You're starting to learn that at Stewart Industries we believe in mixing business with pleasure."

Shondra felt a stab of guilt in her chest. Their words implied that she'd be at Stewart Industries for years to come. But her job there was only meant to be temporary. Now her goals and priorities were muddied by the fact that she had fallen completely in love with Connor. And even though they hadn't exchanged the words with each other, she knew without asking that he felt the same.

Would he understand when she explained her hidden agenda for coming to work for his com-pany? Shondra knew she couldn't let the relationship move forward without letting him in on her secrets. She would sit him down for a serious talk as soon as she found a quiet moment.

But there were no quiet moments in the mall as they each picked out CDs to complete the other's musical education. And she hadn't wanted to spoil their meal as they dined at Le Cirque restaurant in their hotel.

Then the next thing she knew, they were kicking up their heels at the Pure nightclub until four in the morning. And with the typical, go-all-night fervor that Las Vegas inspires, they tumbled into the casinos to play slot machines into well after sunrise. After another all-you-can-eat brunch they fell into bed to sleep until late afternoon.

Shondra awoke around three feeling completely disoriented. Raising her heavy head from the pillow, she glared at Connor, who came from the bathroom looking no worse for wear. "It's only been two days and I feel like I've been in Las Vegas for a week."

He walked over to the phone. "I've got the perfect remedy for that overpartied feeling you're having."

Shondra shook her head. "I can't think of one thing that will make me feel better right now."

"Bloody Marys—"

Shondra winced.

"—and a couple's massage by the pool."

She smiled, letting her head fall back to the pillow. She couldn't argue with that.

After their massages, Shondra and Connor spent a leisurely afternoon in their suite doing almost nothing. It was such a comfort for Shondra to see that she and Connor could enjoy each other's company when there weren't private jets and expensive toys involved.

While Connor left the suite briefly to fill up the ice bucket, Shondra checked her messages. There were three text messages from Tyson and two from Malcolm. Apparently, her father's driver, Joe Dennis, had gone missing. Fear stabbed Shondra's heart for a moment, then she relaxed. They didn't have any proof of foul play. And, from her end, she could at least clear Connor's name. Typing quickly with her thumbs, she sent them both the same message.

I haven't been able to find anything on the company. Investigating Stewart Industries is probably a dead end.

Turning off her phone, she shoved it back into her purse. With a heavy sigh, she decided that when she returned to Houston she was going to tell her family about Connor. If she was going to expect him to understand her situation, she had to be able to come out into the open with their relationship.

That evening they watched television and ordered room service for dinner. Shondra knew there would be no better time to talk to Connor than now. If for no other reason than to finally eliminate the sick-to-her-stomach feeling that rose every time she thought about it.

In the grand scheme of things, Shondra really believed that Connor would be understanding. He had a clear picture of the impact family expectations could have on a person. Her father's death and her desperate need to find out the truth about it would be something he could sympathize with.

And once she'd made it clear that she always gave her full attention to her obligations at Stewart Industries, despite her taking the job with a hidden agenda, then she might even be able to convince him to help her.

"Connor," she started, feeling her heart pounding in her chest. "I think we should talk about our relationship."

He put down his glass of wine and muted the sound on the television, giving her his full attention. With his ice-blue gaze pinning her intently, Shondra was tempted to chicken out.

"When I took this job with Stewart Industries, I had no idea that we were going to—"

A smile spread across his face and he reached out to grab her hands. "No one ever sets out to start an affair with their boss, Shondra. I know I told you that we should decide on our relationship at the end of our time together. But if you're going to give me bad news, I don't want to spoil the last few hours I have with you."

That made Shondra pause. Would he consider what she had to say bad news? She knew Connor didn't want to hear that she wouldn't see him again. At least she could reassure him on that front. "I don't have any bad news about our relationship. I would really like to give us a chance, but there are still those complications that we've been avoiding."

"If you're worried about work, don't be. I know everyone, especially my father, will be surprised when they find out about us. But they'll get over it."

Shondra's spine snapped straight. He was talking about going public. Considering his tenuous relationship with his father, that would be a bold move. "But your father already made it clear that he doesn't want you involved with me."

"My father thinks that he can control me by holding the title of CEO over my head. The fact is, I own forty-nine percent of the company no matter what he does and I'll inherit the other fifty-one percent when he dies. He can keep a hold on the reins for now, if he chooses to, but he can't control them forever. And I'm tired of jumping through hoops for him. He's going to have to face the fact that I'm capable of making smart decisions for myself *and* for the future of the company."

"But, Connor, what if he decides to disinherit you?"

"He'd have to leave fifty-one percent of the company to a stranger, or worse, a bunch of stockholders. He'd never let that happen. As for personal finances, I have my own money now."

"I think that *sounds* great, but will you be able to live with the reality of your father's disapproval? Like I said, he made it pretty clear that he didn't want you involved with me."

Understanding dawned in his eyes. "Oh, you

think— Shondra, my father didn't tell you he didn't want us involved because of you personally. He's not prejudiced. He just wants the opportunity to handpick my wife. Which is ridiculous, and once Valerie announces her marriage and pregnancy—"

"There's still the chance that her father will block that marriage somehow."

Connor grinned. "No, there isn't. I got a text message from Valerie last night. She and Alejandro stayed in Vegas and eloped. She claims that she'd gladly abandon her inheritance to be with him."

"Wow, that's very…romantic?"

"Yes, so you see? Everything is falling into place. I'm not saying everything's going to be easy, but I hope you can see that it will be worth it."

"I can see that. But that's one of the things we should talk about. My family is very close and they've been in mourning over my father. That's made my brothers more overprotective than usual. I think there's a strong possibility that they'll have a problem with our relationship."

"Just give them time to get to know me. They'll figure out that we're made for each other. And that I'd never do anything to hurt you."

"Yes, but, Connor, that's not the only prob—"

"I don't want to talk about the problems anymore," he said, cutting her off with a kiss planted firmly on her mouth.

Running his hands down her torso, he reached for the hem of her shirt and pulled it up over her head. "We have all the time in the world when we get back to Houston to work out our problems. Right now, I want to enjoy our time."

Chapter 14

Connor was on top of the world as he pulled into Shondra's driveway. He was finally beginning to think his life was back on track. Deciding to move out from under his father's wing had been incredibly liberating. Now he was ready to take on whatever the world had in store for him.

Shondra turned to look at him as he turned off the car. "Will you come inside with me?"

He grinned. "I'd love to. But I'm actually expected at my father's this evening. He and I have a lot to talk about."

"Do you have a few minutes? I've really been

wanting to talk to you, and I don't want to put it off any longer."

He leaned across the seat and pressed a kiss against her lips. "I'm sorry, honey. I know I promised you we'd talk. Why don't I come by after I leave my father's place tonight? Would that be okay?"

She smiled at him. "That would be perfect."

Connor got out of the car and followed Shondra to the door, dropping her bag beside her. "I'll see you later tonight," he said, leaning forward to kiss her goodbye.

Shondra wrapped her arms around his neck and Connor was just about to deepen the kiss when he heard yelling. Pulling back, he looked over to see two angry men charging toward him from a parked car in front of Shondra's house.

"Get your hands off my sister," one of them was shouting.

Connor backed away from Shondra with his hands up. "It's okay. It's okay. I'm Connor. Connor Stewart—Shondra's boyfriend."

Both men were on them now. Shondra was buzzing around, trying to get her brothers to calm down. But the shorter of the two barked, "Connor Stewart?"

"You don't understand. We're serious about each other," Connor tried to explain.

The man laughed in his face. "You must be out of your mind. The only reason Shondra had anything to do with you and your company in the first place was to find out what the hell you all have to do with our father's accident. And until you can prove you didn't have anything to do with it, there's no way Shondra would ever get involved with you."

Connor's hands dropped to his sides and his jaw gaped open. Unable to fully process her brother's words, he turned his gaze to Shondra. All the answers he needed were there in her face.

She had paled and was standing stock-still with her eyes wide and her hand pressed to her mouth in shock. There was guilt in her posture and all over her face.

"So this is true?"

"It's not the way Tyson is making it sound. I did want to find out if there was a connection between your company and our father's death, but—"

Connor felt his temperature spike. "That's ridiculous. How could anyone at Stewart Industries have anything to do with your father's death? If that's what you really believe, go ahead.

You can dig for dirt as deep as you like. I don't care. We have nothing to hide."

"Connor, please let me—"

Shondra's other brother, who seemed just as startled by this turn of events as Shondra, tried to rein things in. "Why don't we go inside and discuss this calmly. There's no need to cause a scene out here in the street."

Suddenly he couldn't bear to look at her any longer. "You can have access to any information you want. But stay away from me. I should be used to getting used by women by now, but I never expected it from you."

"Connor, wait!"

He heard Shondra calling after him but he could barely see past his seething anger. Jumping into his car, he peeled out of the driveway.

Shondra watched Connor's hasty exit in shock. Her brothers were speaking to her but she didn't listen. Instead she ran into the condo and slammed the door in Tyson's face.

He stood outside calling after her for a few minutes, but then she heard Malcolm trying to reason with him. After a few minutes the two of them disappeared.

All Shondra could do was sink to the floor in front of the door, barely noticing as tears began to slip from her eyes.

As Connor sped away from Shondra's house, he could barely see straight. In retrospect, she *had* been trying to tell him something. But that wasn't enough to let her off the hook.

She'd had more than enough time to come clean to him once they'd started sleeping together. She'd knowingly deceived him for all of this time.

As his anger mounted, his foot pressed harder on the gas pedal.

He'd been involved with many women who had used him, the worst of which was Valerie. But he'd known they were capable of such behavior, and he had knowingly taken his chances with them. He'd really believed Shondra was different.

He'd been kidding himself.

As Connor got onto the highway, he remembered that he was expected at his father's. How could he face the old man now? He'd been planning to announce his relationship with Shondra and dare his father to protest.

With all the wind taken out of his sails, he had nothing to say. Punching the steering wheel, Connor realized that nothing had changed. He'd made a decision to stop playing his father's games, and he needed to stick by that. His father had only had power over him because Connor had let him. And that was going to end now.

Just then, Shondra's brother's words drifted back to him. They thought SI had something to do with their father's death. He couldn't think of anything more absurd. He thought a lot of things about his father, but he knew he was an honest businessman. He was dedicated to the thousands of workers SI employed, and his first priority had always been keeping the future of the company stable.

Connor pulled into his father's driveway, with his anger fueling his determination further. This was the last day he was going to let anyone take advantage of him.

Mr. Nice Guy had left the building.

Chapter 15

Shondra stared at the road as she drove. It was amazing how quickly life curved in new directions without warning. In the last two months hers had taken so many sharp turns, she could scarcely find her bearings.

If her father had been alive today, things would have been so much different. She never would have taken that CCO position with Stewart Industries, and she never would have fallen in love with Connor.

Could she honestly say she would take all of that back? If she'd had complete control over her life, Shondra would never veer off course, but then, she'd also never experience any of the wonderful surprises that life could lead her to. She'd learned that much from Connor.

Once again, the winding road of life had set her in a new direction. Suddenly her investigation and all the things she'd spent the past few weeks consumed with seemed secondary to one thing. Her love for Connor. How she'd ever managed to convince herself she'd be better off without him, she'd never know.

At once, he'd become the only thing she really needed to be happy.

After Connor stormed off yesterday, Shondra had been lost. It broke her heart to know that he believed she'd used him for her own agenda. When she'd tried to call to explain herself, she'd repeatedly gotten his voice mail.

How many times could she apologize to a recording?

She'd woken up that morning wondering if she would even be welcome in the offices of Stewart Industries anymore. Until she had a chance to speak with Connor, she'd decided it would be best to take the remaining two days left in the week as personal leave.

Shondra's mind kept replaying a humiliating scenario in which Connor would have her escorted from the building on the arms of two burly security officers, throwing her and her belongings into the street.

Their relationship had been a secret. Shondra prayed whatever he wanted to do next—dump her, fire her or both—would be a secret, too.

Today, the road she drove took her back home. She'd spent the night crying on Lisa's shoulder and finding no comfort in the steaming plate of empanadas her friend had made for her. She needed a different kind of comfort. There were some times in life when only a mother's love would do.

Unable to find her mother in the house, Shondra ventured out back to the garden. Despite the fact that the Braddocks had always maintained a landscaper on the grounds, her mother kept a little patch of land with flowers and herbs that she liked to tend to herself.

Sure enough, this is where Shondra found her. Evelyn Braddock must have known something was wrong the minute she looked into Shondra's face, because she'd been kneeling in the soil, but immediately came to her feet when Shondra approached, dropping her gardening gloves and dusting herself off. "Shondra, honey, what's wrong?"

Feeling her throat constrict and unshed tears welling in her eyes, Shondra went into her mother's arms. "I've made a mess of things."

Her mother's arms came around her in a tight squeeze, and Shondra let all the feelings she'd been trying to contain flow free. "I think I've ruined my only chance at love, Mom. I blew it."

Once Shondra had pulled herself together a bit, her mother slipped her arm through her daughter's and said, "Come on, let's walk."

It was a warm fall day and an early rain had knocked off some of the noon heat. Shondra let her mother pull her along the hedged path, while she tried to calm her thoughts with breaths of fresh air.

"First of all, little girl, there's never only one chance at love," Evelyn finally said. "And, if you find the right person, there's a good chance you can fix it. Even if you think you've blown it."

"I wouldn't be so sure about that," Shondra said as she began to confide in her mother. "I took the job at Stewart Industries because the boys and I have reason to believe that Dad's death wasn't an accident."

It was clear that Shondra's mother was surprised by this news, but to her credit, she listened to her daughter's story without interruption.

"—and when he saw us kissing," Shondra finished, "Tyson blurted out the real reason I took the job. He made Connor think there wasn't any possibility that I could have real feelings for him."

Having circled the grounds, Evelyn led Shondra back to the patio and sat across from her. "Shondra, I always knew that one day you would fall in love, and that it would be amazing."

"Does it surprise you that I fell in love with a white man, Mom?"

"His color isn't what matters. What matters is that he makes you happy."

Shondra felt a heaviness lift from her heart. "He does. Connor makes happier than I ever thought I could be."

"That's the way it was when I met your father. Our relationship wasn't always perfect, but the good times always outweighed the bad. And as for the bad times…we got through them."

Shondra nodded. What she had with Connor was worth fighting for. Would he be able to forgive her?

And even if he could, would he fit in with her family? As much as she liked to rebel against her brothers' controlling tendencies, she had to admit that she cared about their opinions.

"Tyson said some horrible things to Connor. I don't know where Malcolm stands, but I don't know if either of them would approve of our relationship."

"I'll handle Tyson and Malcolm," her mother promised. "And I'll handle any snide or racist remarks that may come up about your relationship. But you have to make peace with Connor on your own, love. If his feelings for you are real, he'll come around."

Shondra sat up straighter, feeling more hopeful.

"And in the meantime," her mother continued, "I don't want to hear any more about this undercover business. If you kids have questions about your father's death, then we'll hire a P.I. But I *will not* have any more of my children playing investigator."

As Shondra drove back home that evening, she felt more clearheaded than she had in weeks. Connor had gone out on a limb for her more than once. Now it was her turn to convince him that she was worth gambling his heart on.

* * *

Saturday afternoon, Shondra was laid out on her bed, reading. She'd been forced to find something that would distract her from the gut-wrenching heartbreak that followed her around. Despite her best efforts to reach him, Connor was still avoiding her.

Without warning, Lisa barged into her room, carrying a tray of coffees.

Startled at the interruption, Shondra hurried to shove the book she was reading under her pillow. But she wasn't quick enough to dodge Lisa's caffeine-honed gaze.

"What's that? What are you hiding? Let me see." She set the tray of coffee on Shondra's nightstand and leaped onto the bed, rooting around under the pillows until she'd retrieved *Love's Tender Touch*.

"Aha! You've been reading my romance novels. That's great. You didn't have to hide it from me. You can borrow them anytime. In fact, if you like that one, then you should definitely try *Tantalizing Temptress*. It's about—"

"Hey, slow down there, Lisa. My brain doesn't work as fast as your mouth. How many coffees have you had today?"

"Just two. And I brought some home for you. I didn't know whether or not you wanted a caramel-mocha latte, iced cappuccino or Italian roast, so I brought all three. I'll drink whichever ones you don't want."

"Don't you think you've had enough? As much as I love the free coffee perks, you've been completely wired since you started work as a barista. Are you even sleeping at night?"

Lisa collapsed against Shondra's pillows. "Very fitfully. I have three interviews next week at law firms. Now that I've seen a bit of the world, I know I'll be a better lawyer. And I'll be able to appreciate the structure rather than feel like a slave to it."

Shondra stared at her friend wide-eyed. "Wow. Good for you. I have to admit, I'm a bit surprised. I thought you enjoyed being more of a free spirit."

"Being a free spirit was all well and good, but being broke isn't. Enjoy that coffee because you're going to have to consider it a down payment on the rent until I get a job that pays a living wage."

Shondra laughed, choosing the iced cappuccino from the tray. "No problem. I've got you covered. I'm just glad to know you've finally figured out what you want."

Lisa's face sobered. "What about you? Any word from Connor yet?"

Shondra shook her head. "No, and I'm getting really frustrated. I've read three of your romance novels and the hero always forgives the heroine for her crazy antics. I don't know why real life can't be as simple."

"Real life isn't as simple, but I think you can get some tips from romance novels. For instance, the hero always makes a grand gesture to prove to the heroine that he's changed. Connor's done some over-the-top things to impress you. Maybe he's looking for a woman who can sweep him off *his* feet once in a while."

"Whoa," Shondra shrieked, after thinking about that for a few minutes. "You may be onto something. I have an idea, but I'm going to need to call Connor's assistant to see if she can help me arrange it."

Jumping off the bed, Shondra reached for the phone. She needed to show Connor that she could be just as spontaneous as he was.

Sunday night Connor reclined in his leather lounge chair, trying to find something to watch on television. Just as he'd settled on an eighties movie he'd once loved, the phone was ringing again. The caller ID displayed Shondra's phone number.

His hand reached out to pick it up, and he forced himself to turn away. She'd been telling him for weeks that their lives were too complicated to fit together. It was time he finally started to believe it.

His father had been impressed when Connor finally stood up to him. During their conversation they'd come to an understanding. Connor needed more autonomy to implement more of his new ideas. And Carl had his own reasons for holding on to the company reins a bit longer. From now on, they would both try to be more respectful of the other. Now that he'd taken a stand, he couldn't make a mockery of that by running back to Shondra. He felt like a fool for the way he'd chased her.

Flipping the television channels once again, Connor heard a knock at the door. He knew it couldn't be Shondra; she was probably still talking to his voice mail, he thought bitterly.

Jerking open the door, he saw her two brothers standing on the other side and nearly slammed it closed again. The taller of the two held the door open before he could.

"You have every reason to throw us out of here, but I'm hoping you'll at least hear us out first," the man said.

Rolling his eyes, Connor backed away from the door. The only way he'd get any rest was to get this over with. He had an early flight the next morning, and he couldn't afford to let them bang on his door all night.

"I'm Malcolm Braddock and this is my younger brother, Tyson," the tall one said, referring to the scowling man in the suit beside him.

"We're here because we need to apologize for the scene that took place in front Shondra's house a few days ago."

Tyson, still scowling, leveled his gaze at Connor. "I shouldn't have said what I did to you. I didn't know all the facts when I lashed out. That's a problem I'm still trying to work on."

Connor shrugged. "Fine," he said, anxious to send them on their way. "If that's all… I accept and good night."

Malcolm held up his hand to stop Connor from crossing to the door. "That's not really all. We know that you and Shondra aren't speaking right now, and that's our fault. More than likely, until the two of you make up, she won't ever speak to us again."

Connor shook his head. "I'm sorry, but that's not something I can help you with."

"I know you don't know us, and probably have no desire to discuss your love life with strangers. But if Shondra wasn't completely honest with you about her role at Stewart Industries, at least let us explain why."

Reluctantly, Connor showed them to the sofa and sat down to listen.

Ducking behind the curtain at the back of Connor's jet, Shondra had to resist the urge to peek out the small window again. He would be arriving soon, and she had to get ready.

She fumbled with the champagne bottle, spilling it all over the tray as she tried to pour some into a flute of orange juice. Her hands trembled violently with both anticipation and fear.

Taking a deep breath, Shondra cleaned up her mess and started again. Connor's breakfast had to be perfect—a red rose at full bloom in a bud vase, a mimosa, black coffee and a fresh platter of croissants and fruit.

Her entire future was riding on the next few minutes going according to plan. She, Lisa and Sarah had put their heads together and had come up with a plan to ambush Connor. At 30,000 feet in the air, he wouldn't be able to avoid her. She'd finally have her shot at getting through to him.

Five minutes later, Shondra heard Connor board the plane. He exchanged a few words with the pilot then settled himself in one of the big leather chairs.

Shondra had arranged to take the place of Rosie, Connor's usual flight attendant. Dressed in Rosie's navy-blue pencil skirt, a red pin-striped blouse and navy vest, Shondra was ready to offer Connor some in-flight service.

Hunkered behind the curtain, time dragged by as Shondra battled clammy palms and heart palpitations while waiting for the plane to level out in the air.

Finally, willing her legs not to buckle beneath her, she walked up the aisle carrying Connor's tray. "Are you ready for your breakfast, Mr. Stewart?" Shondra heard her voice shaking with nerves as she placed the tray in front of him.

Connor looked up at her and gasped. "Shondra? Is that you? What are you doing—"

Afraid of losing her nerve, Shondra held her finger to his lips to pause his questions. "Wait. Before you say anything, please just let me say what I came here to tell you."

Slipping into the seat facing him, she leaned forward, locking onto his gaze. "I know you're feeling used and betrayed right now, but it was never my intention to make you feel that way. When I took the CCO position at SI, I had no idea I was going to fall in love with you."

"Shondra, I—"

"Just listen, please." Shondra went on to explain to Connor about Gloria tracing a number found in her father's phone logs back to SI and the anonymous phone call that started them on the investigation into Harmon Braddock's death.

Connor listened with an anxious look that sent Shondra's heart sinking. Maybe she wasn't getting through to him after all.

"As you can imagine, my family had no idea who we could trust, but given the links to SI, I felt that I had to check out the company myself. Recently my father's office was trashed, and while I was working at SI, the anonymous caller contacted me again telling me to keep looking. Just in the last couple of days my father's driver has gone missing."

"Shondra, you don't—"

Shondra rushed to continue, feeling that she was losing him. "I always wanted to confide in you, Connor, but I knew my brothers wouldn't approve. Trying to please your family is a hard habit to break, and I know you know that first-hand—"

Finally, Connor grabbed her hands and squeezed them hard. "Shondra, you can stop. I love you, too. And I forgive you. In fact, if you'd let me get a word in edgewise, I could have told you that I already know all of this."

"*What?* How could you know?"

"I had some visitors at my apartment last night."

Shondra stared at him blankly. "Who?"

"Your brothers, Tyson and Malcolm. They wanted to apologize for running me off. They felt the need to explain the situation so that you would forgive them. They may have been hard on you at times, but they really love you and want what's best for you. Apparently they think that's me."

Shondra's eyes went wide. "You're kidding me, right? My brothers actually came to talk to you? They gave us their blessing?"

"Yes, they did. I would have told you myself but, as you see, I had an early flight this morning. I was going to call you from Brazil and apologize for shutting you out. I should have answered your calls."

Shondra looked down at her uniform, shaking her head. "Wow, so all of this was for nothing."

"I wouldn't say that. I think it proves you've learned your lesson. In the future, if you want something from me, all you have to do is ask. I had no idea you thought your father's death wasn't an accident. But, if someone at SI knows anything about this, you can count on my help. You can have the phone logs, and we can question anyone you think might know something about this."

Shondra squeezed Connor's fingers. "Thank you, Connor. This means the world to me and my family."

"So we're making it official then? You and I are a couple. No more secrets. Our relationship is out in the open, and we don't care who knows about it, right?"

"That's right," Shondra said, giggling.

"Great. Now on to more important business," he said, swiveling in his seat and holding open his arms. "Come here. That flight attendant uniform looks sexy on you. I want to take it off."

Shondra settled herself on his lap, but pushed his roving hands away from her buttons. "Not so fast. You've got plenty of time for that. It's a long flight to Brazil."

Connor fixed her with his wicked grin. "Have you ever been to Brazil?"

"Nope."

"You're going to love it. When I'm finished with business, we'll fly to Rio. They have the best nude beaches."

She gasped. "Nude beaches?"

"Yes, and skinny-dipping. Have you ever been skinny-dipping?"

"Nope."

"Stick with me, babe. I've got so much to show you," Connor said, pressing a long sweet kiss against her lips.

All work and no play…

SUITE
Temptation

Acclaimed Author
ANITA
BUNKLEY

When Riana Cole kissed Andre Preaux goodbye to conquer
the San Antonio business world, Andre had given up without
a fight. Now, years later, they are reunited, and memories
of delicious passion come flooding back. Andre is
determined to get her back, but this time he's negotiating
for one thing only—her heart.

"Anita Bunkley's descriptive winter scenery, likable,
well-written characters and engaging story make
Suite Embrace very entertaining."
—*Romantic Times BOOKreviews*

Available the first week of September wherever books are sold.

KIMANI™
ROMANCE

www.kimanipress.com

KPAB0800908

For All We Know

NATIONAL BESTSELLING AUTHOR

SANDRA KITT

Michaela Landry's quiet summer of
house-sitting takes a dramatic turn when
she finds a runaway teen and brings him
to the nearest hospital. There she meets
Cooper Smith Townsend, a local pastor
whose calm demeanor and dedication are
as attractive as his rugged good looks.
Now their biggest challenge will be to trust
that a passion neither planned for is strong
enough to overcome any obstacle.

*Coming the first week of September 2008,
wherever books are sold.*

ARABESQUE®

www.kimanipress.com

KPSKI040908

Where there's smoke, there's fire!

MAKE IT
HOT

Gwyneth Bolton

Brooding injured firefighter Joel Hightower's only hope
to save his career is sassy physical therapist Samantha
Dash. But as the sizzling attraction between them
intensifies, Samantha must decide whether a future with
surly Joel is worth the threat to her career.

The Hightowers
**Four brothers on a mission
to protect, serve and love.**

Available the first week of September wherever books are sold.

KIMANI™
ROMANCE

www.kimanipress.com   KPGB0830908